Sky Eyes

Sherry Derr-Wille

HAVE BOOKS - WILL TRAVEL
AUTOGRAPHED
AUTHOR COPY

Published by Rogue Phoenix Press, LLP
Copyright © 2018

Names, characters and incidents depicted in this book are products of the author's imagination or are used fictitiously. Any resemblance to actual events, locales, organizations, or persons, living or dead, is entirely coincidental and beyond the intent of the author or the publisher. No part of this book may be reproduced or transmitted in any form or by any means, electronic or mechanical, including photocopying, recording, or by any information storage and retrieval system, without permission in writing from the publisher.

ISBN: 978-1986327138

Credits
Cover Artist: Designs by Ms G
Editor: Amanda Armstrong

Dedication

To my readers and fans as well as my crazy imagination.

CHAPTER ONE

Morning Star's breasts hung heavy with milk. Just six suns ago she'd given birth to twins and her body was now producing enough milk for both babies. In the night, the spirit of death came and took one of the babies to the land of the ancestors leaving only one child to drain her breasts of their heaviness.

Even though she mourned the passing of her daughter, she knew there was still work to be done. Now, with her husband, Running Deer, at her side and her son strapped to her back, she walked toward the river looking for the edible plants to be harvested and dried to be used during the coming winter.

Off to one side, she heard the cries of a child. "Did you hear that?"

"I did, but it is nothing we should concern ourselves with. There is a white settler's cabin close by and it is possible they have a child. It is only calling for its mother."

The wails of the child became louder and Morning Star couldn't help but stray from her husband's side to investigate.

The cabin of the white settlers was constructed of logs and looked very strange to Morning Star. The cries of the infant from inside the cabin grew louder and more demanding. Knowing she shouldn't go any further,

Morning Star continued to walk toward the cabin to investigate.

Inside she saw a very young woman lying on a raised bed, her breaths sounding shallow. The babe had been placed beside her and screamed her protests because of an empty belly, at least that was what Morning Star thought.

The white woman opened her eyes, but showed no fear. To Morning Star's surprise, the woman spoke to her in her own tongue.

"My name is Martha and this is my baby. I am dying."

"How is it you speak my language?"

"My husband, Robert, was trained and sent to this area to minister to the tribes. He taught me. Unfortunately, he was killed in an accident several moons ago. He is buried behind the cabin. Now I will be joining him. Will you take my daughter? Her name is Kathryn."

The words Martha spoke seemed to have drained all of her strength. She closed her eyes and almost immediately her breathing stopped.

As though to protest the loss of her mother the baby cried even louder than before.

"What are you doing in here woman?"

Morning Star turned at the sound of her husband's voice.

"The woman, Martha, spoke to me in our language. She said her husband was killed and is buried in the back of the cabin. Now she has joined him in death. She begged me to take her child. I think it is best if we bury her beside her husband. When the task is done, burn this cabin."

"How could she speak in our language?"

"She said she was trained to speak our language because her husband was to minister to our people. I do not understand the meaning of this, but I cannot leave this child to die when I have more than enough milk for two babies."

Running Deer shook his head. "You make sense, but what will the others say about us taking a white child into our midst?"

"I do not care. Don't you think the Great Spirit has sent her to us to replace the daughter the spirit of death took from me in the night? She needs me as much as I need her."

"Of course, you are right. I will bury the woman beside her husband. Once I have finished, I will burn the cabin. If we are going to take this child, what will we call her?"

Morning Star picked up the crying child, giving her comfort. Once the crying stopped, the child looked at her in wonder. "Her mother called her Katheryn. Of course, that is not a name of our people. Just look at her eyes. They are the color of the sky. I will call her Sky Eyes."

With the baby properly named, Morning Star bared her breast and allowed the child to take her engorged nipple into her mouth. While she nursed the baby, Running Deer prepared the woman for burial. He took several of the items from the cabin to put into the grave with her. After wrapping Martha in one of the blankets, he handed another to Morning Star.

She smiled her thanks. Until she could return to her home and retrieve the cradleboard she had thought would go unused, she could carry the baby in the blanket.

Morning Star sat in the sun and nursed her son while Sky Eyes slept. From behind the cabin, she could hear her husband preparing the grave for the woman and her belongings. She knew he would bury her with the same traditions he had used to bury their daughter earlier in the day. What started as a day of sorrow for Morning Star had turned into one of joy. She would raise the white woman's child as though it was her own. When Sky Eyes was old enough, she would tell her of her white mother who entrusted her daughter to a strange woman in order to spare her life. When she told her of all of this, she would also give her back her white name of Kathryn.

Her eyes were becoming heavy when Running Deer returned to the front of the cabin. "I see both children are contently sleeping. It is almost time for us to return to the village. Have you thought of how you will explain this child when people ask where she has come from?"

"I will tell them the truth. The Great Spirit saw my anguish over losing my daughter to the spirit of death. While the spirit of death waited to claim this child's mother, he sent me to rescue the child and raise it as my own."

"I pray what you are doing is the right thing. I too mourn the loss of our daughter but I am not certain how our people will react to this white child. She is innocent, but I have heard terrible stories of what the whites have done to the tribes to the east of us."

Although Running Deer told her he intended to burn down the cabin, he left it intact when it was time to return to the village.

"Are you not going to burn the cabin?"

"I will do it later. For now, we must return to our home. The sun is going down and I do not want to put you or the children in danger. There are animals in the forest who could hurt you badly. It is best if we return to the village. Besides, this child was present when her mother died. We do not know how much a child remembers, but her day has been hard. It is not proper for her to be present when I burn the house that was meant to be her home."

Morning Star agreed with her husband. She did not want this new daughter to harbor dark memories of, not only the death of her natural mother, but also, the loss of the home her parents worked so hard to build to shelter her from birth to when she became a woman.

~ * ~

Once they returned to their lodge, the woman everyone called Old Grandmother greeted them. "I knew it. I knew the Great Spirit would look kindly upon you this day. When I heard you mourning the loss of your girl child, I prayed to the Great Spirit to give you comfort. Not long after my prayer I had a vision of you finding a cabin of a white settler in the forest. I saw you go into the cabin and rescue this child from the horrors of the death of her mother. Seeing you return to this village as a complete family I know the vision from the Great Spirit was right and true."

"I, too, believe the Great Spirit sent me to the cabin to rescue this child as a replacement for my own daughter. Had I not heard her cries of hunger, I would have never gone into the cabin. With her final breath, her mother begged me to take her child and raise her as my own. She also told me the child's name is Kathryn but I have named her Sky Eyes. I will hold her white name in my heart and when the time is right, I will tell her of her origins and the woman who loved her enough to entrust her care to a stranger."

CHAPTER TWO

Sky Eyes knew she was different from the other children in the village, different even from her brother, Otter Pup. The skin beneath her clothing was white rather than brown, her hair was not black, but brown with red streaks when the sun hit it right. The most important difference was the fact her eyes were the color of the sky, lending their color to her name. Although her friends noticed her differences, they never teased her about them. She was accepted for who and what she was.

When she was old enough to question the differences, her mother insisted her appearance was a gift from the Great Spirit. As a child, she accepted the explanation but as she became a woman, she wondered if there was something Morning Star wasn't telling her.

"Sky," her mother called. "I need your help."

Sky set aside her thoughts about her differences and hurried to her mother's side. From the corner of her eye she caught a glimpse of her brother. Otter was preparing to go hunting with their father. She wished she could go hunting rather than do the woman's work her mother planned for her.

"What can I help you with, Mother?" she asked as soon as she stood beside her mother at the cooking fire.

"I would like you to come with me to the river. It is spring and I know there will be many plants for us to pick to enhance our meals and use in the midwives' lodge. This is always my favorite time of the year. It was in the spring when both you and your brother were born."

Sky never tired of hearing her mother tell of how she gave birth to two babies at the same time. It amazed her how her mother carried two children within her now slender body.

They walked in silence until they came to the river. "I brought you here for a special reason today. You have recently become a woman and soon some of the young men will begin to court you. I know there is one special young man who has already spoken to your father. Before the time comes, I must tell you about your birth."

"I know how you carried Otter and me in your belly until it was time for us to be born. What else is there for me to know?"

"There is much," Morning Star replied as she turned away from the river. "I did give birth to two babies, a boy and a girl. When they were six suns old, the spirit of death came and claimed my daughter. I still had Otter, but my heart was heavy. After your father buried the baby, we came to this area of the river to hunt for spring greens. We had just arrived when I heard the cries of a very young baby. Running Deer said not to investigate, but I could not help myself. What I found was a woman dying of childbirth fever. We were surprised because she was white but she spoke our language. She begged me to take her child and not to let her die. You are the baby I found in the cabin. I stayed with your mother until she drew her final breath."

"Are you saying you are not my real mother?" Sky Eyes asked, hardly able to believe the story her mother just told her.

"In all aspects, I am your real mother. I have suckled you at my breast and cared for you when you were sick. You were not born of my body, but your white mother entrusted you to my care. She knew she was dying. With her last breath, she asked me to take you as my own and raise you to be a fine woman. She also told me your real name was Kathryn. Since it was a white name your father and I called you Sky Eyes. It described you perfectly."

Sky Eyes mouthed the white name. It sounded alien in her mind and she didn't know if she would be able to put voice to the name her white mother had given her. "Can you show me where this cabin was? Do you know where my white mother is buried?"

"The answer to both of your questions is yes. We are not far from the cabin as well as the graves of your white mother and father. It is the reason I have brought you here today."

Sky Eyes looked around the area. Nothing seemed familiar to her. Unable to think of anything to say, she allowed her mother to lead her to a clearing in the forest not far from the swollen stream.

As soon as they stepped into the grassy area, she saw two pieces of wood standing guard over a place where the earth had sunken in.

"These are the graves of your white parents. The wood was there when we arrived and designated the grave of your white father. Running Deer noticed it and placed your white mother beside him. He was unsure as to how to properly bury her, so he buried her using our customs. He wrapped her in a blanket from the bed where we found her, along with several of her possessions."

Sky Eyes knelt beside the wooden stick and ran her fingers over the strange markings. She was certain at one time they were easy to read, but now they were nothing more than shadows of what they were originally.

"Do you know how they died?"

"Your mother, her name was Martha. She said your father, Robert, was sent here to minister to the people. Martha told me Robert was killed in an accident and she was left alone to carry on. I fear she died of childbirth fever."

Sky Eyes nodded her head. "How was she able to speak to you? I have heard the whites speak a language none of us can understand."

"You must listen to me more closely. I told you she spoke our language. She said she was taught to speak it before they came here. Had things been different they might have come to our village to tell of the white man's God."

Sky Eyes remembered when a white man came to speak with the elders. Using hand signs, he told the elders he wanted to teach them of his God. From what she'd been told, their chief asked the man to leave the people alone. Although there had been no hostilities, the unarmed man was outnumbered by the men of the village, each of whom was armed with bows as well as knives. Had her white father lived would he have been met with the same hostilities?

She knelt in the lush spring grass next to the sticks with the strange markings. *This is the grave of my white father. If things had been different would he have been able to give me the love I have lived with all my life?*

Even knowing her white mother lay buried next to her white father, the pull of her mother's resting place was nowhere near as strong as that of the grave marked by the sticks. She knew it was probably because the land reclaimed the area that had been disturbed by the digging of the grave. It had also reclaimed the area covering her white father, but had not taken away the sticks.

After several minutes of silent contemplation of everything her mother told her this day, she finally got to her feet and looked to where her mother stood.

"You spoke of a cabin. Where is it? I see nothing that looks like somewhere a white settler would live."

"On that day, your father, Running Deer, came back to the village with me. Days later, he went back to the cabin and burned it to the ground. He certainly didn't want other whites to come into the area and live in the cabin. He felt the cabin to be a sacred place because it was where you were born and he wanted no one else to live there."

Sky Eyes scanned the area looking for signs of what was once a white man's cabin, the cabin of her parents. Perhaps it was the place where she had been conceived and definitely where she had been born. Like the graves, the grass had reclaimed the area leaving no hint of what was once a happy home.

"I see nothing here," she lamented.

"The land always reclaims its own. I am certain your white parents loved you very much. Why else would your mother have entrusted your care and upbringing to me? I think that day I was led to the white man's lodge where you were born by the Great Spirit so your life could be saved."

Sky Eyes accepted what her mother said. As she contemplated it she knelt in the lush prairie grass and ran her hands over the sticks marking the grave of her white father. "What is the meaning of these sticks?"

"Your father and I asked the same question. As you know your father has joined several hunting parties. While he was with one of those groups, the men were talking about the white men who came to their villages. They told him the white missionaries taught them of their God. The symbol of this God is crossed sticks like those marking the grave of your white father. I believe your mother was a highly religious person and marked her husband's grave with the sign of their God. At the time we buried your mother, we knew nothing of this and so we did not mark her grave in such a way. I am sorry for that, but I do not think her God would hold it against her."

"Do I look like her?"

"I'm certain you do, but you must remember, I saw her only for a short time before her death. When I look at you, I see only my daughter, Sky Eyes."

The wind picked up and in the distance there was a roll of thunder. "I fear if we stay here much longer, we will be caught in the storm. If that were the case your father and brother will worry about us."

Sky Eyes laughed at her mother's words. "I think they would miss the food we would be preparing for them more than they would miss us. Men think only of their stomachs."

"You are older than your years. I know they love us. Unfortunately, they are men and that's not a feeling men want others to see in them. Men don't want to admit to the fact that without their women they are nothing. It is a secret among women knowing we are the stronger ones and it is wise not to allow our men to know it."

Together they laughed as they walked through the forest toward their village. In her heart, Sky Eyes knew she would return to the place of her birth as well as the graves of her white parents in the future.

~ * ~

Over the next few weeks the seasons turned from spring to summer.

While the men hunted, the women tended their gardens. From them, they were able to dry and store the fruits and vegetables for the winter that was certain to come.

Although Sky Eyes often thought of the grave with its strange sticks, summer was such a busy time, she did not return.

By the end of the summer, Hunting Hawk, Otter's man name, was now old enough to go on the big hunts with the men. Before his vision quest he'd gone hunting with his father but was not allowed to go with the other men. Along with the men he brought much game into the village and Sky Eyes worked with the other women to prepare it as they did the fruits and vegetables, in order to sustain the people through the long winter that stretched before them.

It was evening and Sky Eyes helped her mother clean up the remains of their meal. The voices of the men gathered around the fire sounded in her head as they spoke of the hunt they planned for the next morning. She paid little attention until she heard them speak of the white men who had been seen on the far side of the forest. Immediately, she took more of an interest in their conversation.

"I saw many white men by the falls," Stalking Badger said. "They rode horses as we do. Unlike us, they make so much noise as they travel, they frighten away the animals that give us life. Their horse's hooves clatter against the rocks. I do not know how an animal can make so much noise when traveling at a slow walk. I do not like to see these strangers invading our land."

"I am afraid there is nothing we can do to stop them," Angry Otter, the medicine man, commented. "I have had many visions of these white men. Their coming has been prophesized for a long time. I prayed I would never see the day when they arrived but it seems it is our generation who will have to meet and learn to live with them in peace. In my visions, I see them as numerous as the stars in the sky. The days of the people are numbered. We would be wise to welcome them with peace in our hearts."

The other men argued different sides of the question of the newcomers to the land. Their opinions didn't matter to Sky Eyes. What did matter, was these white men were like her. Their skin was white and perhaps their eyes were the same color as hers. What would it be like to see someone who looked more like her than the people she'd known all her life?

"I do not like the sound of the conversation of the men," Morning Star said. "It sounds as though they are thinking of calling a war counsel. Why can't they listen to Mad Beaver? He makes sense. There is much land, enough for all."

"How many of those men know that I am white?" Sky Eyes inquired. "I have never felt hate from anyone in this place where I have grown from infant to woman, but now they talk about those like me as though they are our enemy. Am I also the enemy?"

Morning Star came to where her daughter was sitting and pulled her into an embrace. "You know everyone loves you as your father, brother and I do. It is possible they knew you were white when we first brought you to become part of our family, but they have probably forgotten about it. You are Sky Eyes, beloved daughter and loyal sister. You are loved. No one sees you as the enemy. I don't even know if they think the white men are enemies. Men just like to talk and talk of war is exciting, even if nothing ever comes of it. Do not let their discussions bother you. It has nothing to do with us."

Sky Eyes turned her thoughts inward. *I wish I could believe everything my mother has told me, but in my heart of hearts, I know I'd different. What will happen once I am pledged to a young man and he sees me for what I am. Will he accept me as a member of the people or will he set me aside because beneath my clothes my skin is white like the men who are coming to take away our land? At least that's what the men are saying about them.*

As a child, I ran naked with the other children and my skin became bronzed by the summer sun. Once my mother made me wear clothing all the time, I noticed the skin beneath my clothing becoming paler than that of my brother. Now knowing of my origins, it all makes sense.

CHAPTER THREE

The next morning when the men went hunting and the women left to tend their gardens, Sky Eyes decided it was time for her to go to the graves of her white parents. Without telling anyone of her plans, she took some dried meat and fruit to sustain her while she communed with the spirits of her parents.

Since her mother had taken her to the gravesites she'd learned much more of what her white mother said with her dying breath. Not only had she given her child the name of Kathryn, she told Morning Star her husband's name was Robert and her name Martha. She was able to speak the language of the people and said they had been sent to the area to teach the people about their God.

Sky Eyes loved the Great Spirit, she hung on every word Mad Beaver spoke but she couldn't quiet the inner voice saying there might be more for her with her own people.

Before leaving the village, she looked longingly at the lodge where she had grown from an orphaned infant to a woman ready to take on the tasks of a wife and mother. "I love my family among the people," she whispered to the wind, "but I feel I must see if I can contact the spirits of the people who gave me life."

Leaving the village behind, she walked toward the river, as she had with her mother only months earlier. She made the trip many times in her night time dreams. Because of those dreams, she had no doubts of the path she would take to the graves that were her destination.

Sky Eyes

Above her flew a flock of geese, so large it almost darkened the autumn sky. *Winter is coming soon. This may be the only time I am able to come back to where I was born. Once the snow is deep I will not be able to return until spring. I need to be here today.*

She was so lost in thought, the distance between the village and the long-forgotten graves came into view before Sky Eyes thought she'd walked far enough.

Not knowing exactly where her mother rested, she knelt beside the crossed sticks and placed her hands on the grass that would soon be covered with the snow of winter. Almost immediately she began to have a vision.

In her vision, Sky could see the cabin that once sat not far from the graves. Inside the cabin, she saw furnishings that were alien to her. A beautiful woman with her brown hair braided and wound around her head tended a fire, but not an open one like the women in the village tended. She stirred something in a large cooking pot. Sky Eyes could almost smell the delicious meal the woman was cooking.

From behind the woman a tall man with light hair came up and put his arms around the woman's waist. He spoke in a language Sky Eyes couldn't understand and yet she knew the words he said were ones of love. She could see it in his eyes as well as his actions.

Without warning, the ground beneath her hands began to tremble. As soon as the vision appeared, it dissolved. Before she could thank the Great Spirit for giving her a glimpse of the parents she never saw in life, several horses came into the clearing. Her instincts told her to get to her feet and flee into the woods. Instead she stood rooted to the spot, frozen with fear of the men riding the horses.

~ * ~

Lukas Palmer marveled at the vast prairie land he and his party were riding through. Patches of woodlands broke the endless sea of lush grasses and small lakes, along with rivers and streams provided the life giving water. He knew it would be the perfect place to settle and raise a family.

"I've never seen a more fertile area," Lukas' older brother Marcus said. "I can see us having farms next to each other here."

"I agree, but what about the natives? Do we know if they are hostile or friendly?"

"The people we talked to in New York assured us they are friendly. Thomas says he can even speak some of their language. He said he learned it when his brother, Robert, and his wife, Martha, came out here as missionaries several years ago. He says we are close to where their cabin is. I know he's looking forward to seeing them again, even though he hasn't heard from them since shortly after they built their cabin."

"Marcus is right," Thomas Clay said, joining their conversation. "I am anxious to reconnect with my brother. By this time, they more than likely have several children."

Lukas breathed a sigh of relief. It was entirely possible they wouldn't have to depend upon Thomas to translate for them. If Robert and Martha were ministering to the natives, the people would probably speak English. It made him feel much better just knowing he would be able to be understood when he told them he just wanted to be a good neighbor.

In the distance, he saw something so unexpected he blinked several times to make certain he wasn't experiencing a vision that wasn't there. He finally realized the woman who knelt in the prairie grass was real rather than a mirage. It was evident the others in his group also saw her as they urged their horses forward and quickly surrounded her.

The woman got to her feet and stared at them, fear etched on her face. Although she was dressed in a buckskin dress and knee high moccasins her features belied the fact of white heritage somewhere in her background.

"Martha," Thomas gasped.

"Are you sure?" Lukas questioned.

Thomas shook his head. "My eyes must be playing tricks on me. This woman is much too young to be Martha. Even if it is her, why is she dressed like that and staring at us as though she doesn't understand what we are saying to her?"

Sky Eyes

~ * ~

Sky Eyes knew there was no way for her to escape the white men who now surrounded her. One of the men dismounted and looked at her intently. "Martha," the man said.

For a moment, she thought he spoke her white mother's name, but dismissed the idea as soon as it entered her head. *How can this stranger know the name I only learned months earlier when my mother told me the story of my white parents?*

Why is it that this man looks like the man in my vision? His hair is light and his eyes are as blue as mine.

He took a step forward and began to speak in her language. "My name is Thomas. I come as a friend. By what name are you called?"

Hearing this man speak in her native language caused her to hesitate. Since she had two names, which one should she use. Rather than betray her white heritage she decided to keep the name of Kathryn a secret known only to herself and her mother. "I am called Sky Eyes."

"You look like my brother's wife. That is why I called you Martha. Do you know of white people who live around here and are called Robert and Martha?"

She instinctively looked down at the crossed sticks. This man was talking about her white parents who died before she could say she ever knew them. If this man was Robert's brother, that meant he was her uncle.

"I do not know them. Perhaps my parents..."

"Daughter," Running Deer called before she could finish her answer.

At the sound of his voice, the white men surrounding her turned to face her father. Even to her he looked fierce with his knife at his side and his bow slung over his shoulder. With him was Hunting Hawk. It was evident they had just returned from hunting and came in search of her.

"What is going on here?"

The man who called himself Thomas held out his hand in a gesture to show he held no weapons. "We have come in peace, looking for land to settle on and raise our families."

The look of bewilderment on her father's face as he heard this white man speaking their language mirrored her own. "How is it you speak our language?"

Sky Eyes looked back at Thomas and saw his features begin to relax. "I come from a place far east of here called New York. My brother, Robert, and his wife, Martha, trained to be missionaries and when they did they were taught your language by a man of your people who had been brought east with some of the early explorers of this land. He said it would be best if his people heard our message in their own tongue."

"What do you want with my daughter?"

"We want nothing with her. We saw her alone and only wanted to speak with her and offer her our friendship if she was lost and alone. I see now she is neither lost nor alone. We mean no harm."

Her father nodded and his stance changed from challenging to one of acceptance. "If you mean us no harm, we accept your friendship. I have come only to bring my daughter back to our lodge, as the sun is sinking into the western sky and her mother is worried about her safety."

"We would like to settle in this area. Would you allow us to live close to you in peace?"

"I will speak to our leaders. Having white men living close to us is something that must be discussed. We have hunted these lands since the beginning of time and we want nothing or no one to deny us our right."

"Your rights are ones we are willing to honor. We want nothing more than to farm the land and raise our families."

"We will sit in counsel about this and meet you here when the sun rises for the second time. For now, I will take my daughter home and put her mother's mind at ease."

~ * ~

"Well, if that don't beat all," Thomas said, once the two men left with the young woman. "What is a white girl doing with them?"

"Maybe this might explain it," Lukas replied. "There is a wooden cross here. It has a name carved into the crosspiece. It's weathered, but I can make out a couple of letters, it could say Robert Clay. I just can't be certain."

Thomas knelt next to the cross. Tears formed in his eyes as he ran his hand over the letters carved into the rough wood. The first letter was, indeed, an 'R' and another deeply carved letter was a 'C'. "This could be why I haven't heard from him since he left New York. If I'm not mistaken, Martha also lies beneath the sod. I have a feeling Sky Eyes is my niece. I have no idea how she came to be with the natives, I pray they weren't responsible for the deaths of my brother and his wife."

"I doubt if they were responsible, because if they were they wouldn't have buried them nor would they have made a cross to mark your brother's resting place. I can't believe they would have known his name to say nothing of how to spell it. Was his wife able to read and write?"

Thomas pondered Marcus' question. "Martha's father was a minister and her mother was from a wealthy family. I am certain she was educated. It's entirely possible she buried Robert and carved his name on the cross. What I don't understand is what happened to her. If Sky Eyes is their child, I can only assume she is also dead."

~ * ~

"Why did you not run back to the forest when you saw the white men coming?" Hunting Hawk asked.

"I had no time. I was kneeling in the grass and had a vision. In the middle of the vision, the ground began to shake and when I looked up I was surrounded by those men on their horses. I was surprised when the man named Thomas spoke in our language."

"I don't understand why you came this far from the village without telling anyone where you were going," Hunting Hawk insisted.

"Just as you are now a man, your sister is a woman," Running Deer said. "She has no reason to answer your questions. What she does is her decision. The problem is she didn't tell anyone where she was going or why. I'm certain there is a logical explanation that she will give to your mother and me."

Sky Eyes could tell her father's words shamed her brother. Since he had been on his vision quest he considered himself a man and therefore entitled to ask questions of anyone in the village.

As soon as they entered the village, Sky Eyes saw her mother standing outside of their lodge, an expression of concern etched on her face.

"I am sorry I worried you, Mother. I've been watching the signs and I know winter will soon be upon us. I wanted to visit the graves of my white parents before the snow comes and covers their resting place so I would be unable to find them."

"I heard your response to your brother and I understand how you could have become so easily surrounded," her father commented. "What I want to know is what was the vision you received?"

"I have long pondered the story you and Mother have told me about my white parents as well as the cabin where I was born. As I knelt in front of the sticks denoting my white father's grave, I saw the cabin as well as the furnishings within it. I also saw a woman who I believed was my white mother. I could see traces of my face in her face. She was then joined by a tall white man with light hair and eyes that matched my own. The vision so entranced me I was not aware of the approach of the white men until I felt the earth tremble beneath the hooves of their horses. By the time I saw them, it was too late to flee to the forest."

Her father nodded his head in agreement with what she was saying.

"The man who called himself Thomas said Martha to me, as though he thought that was my name. He then spoke to me in our language and asked about Robert and Martha. I recognized the names as those of my white parents. I also recognized the man, Thomas, as he closely resembled the man in my vision. I am certain he is my white uncle. This is all very confusing to me. Should I have such feelings for a man our people consider an enemy?"

Running Deer embraced his daughter. "I understand your confusion. You are a woman with your feet in two different worlds. You were blessed to have a white mother who knew she was dying. Somehow, she trusted us enough to allow your mother and me to care for you as you grew from infant to woman. I was the one who buried her and grieved her passing. At the same time, I rejoiced because the Great Spirit sent you to us to replace the daughter we lost so soon after her birth. In this village, you have grown to be a wise woman secure in the love of everyone who knows you. Now a new family has come into your life. No one would think less of you if you want to get to know them but I will pray to the Great Spirit you would not forget those of us who have raised and loved you."

"Oh, Father, I will never forget anyone in this village. I would also like to learn more of the people of my birth. These men have said they come in peace and only want to live as good neighbors."

"If we can believe what they say, I have no objections to you getting to know these people. I will meet with the leaders tomorrow and decide what to do concerning these men. When I meet with the men again, I would like to have you and your mother at my side. I am certain the leaders will understand my request when I explain your connection with these men. If this Thomas is indeed your uncle, our people will treat him with the honor reserved for family."

Sky Eyes smiled at her father's words. She prayed the leaders would be receptive to what her father had to say about the white men who were now encroaching upon their land.

CHAPTER FOUR

While her father spoke with the leaders, Sky Eyes prayed to the Great Spirit for guidance where the white strangers were concerned.

"May I talk to you, Sky Eyes?" Sly Coyote asked.

It took a moment for her to realize who was speaking to her. All her life Sly Coyote had been her playmate and recently he asked her father if he could court her.

"Of course you can. We have always been able to speak with one another."

She turned to face him, but his expression worried her. Before, she'd seen love in his eyes, but today his eyes were filled with questions.

"I have heard a rumor and you are the only person who can give me the answer."

Sky Eyes dreaded the words that would be forthcoming from Sly Coyote's mouth. Ever since she met the white men the day before, she worried about how the people would see her once they knew the truth about her birth.

"I know what you have heard, and the answer to your question is yes, I am white. I knew nothing of this until my mother told me the story in the spring and took me to see the graves of the white people who gave me life. Had she not taken pity on an orphaned infant, I would have died with them."

"Maybe it would have been better if you had died with your parents. You know how the people feel about the white men who are invading our lands. Not only did you invade our village, you almost stole my heart. How could you have allowed me to fall in love with you?"

"I allowed nothing. You are the one who fell in love with me, just as I have always loved you. I am no different now that I know the truth of my birth than I was last winter when you asked my father if you could court me."

"Of course you are different. If it were to come to war, would you stand with the people or with the whites? If I were to take you as my wife, would I have to sleep with one eye open for fear of being murdered in my bed because your skin is white and mine is red?"

"Now the words you speak are nonsense. If this is exactly how you feel perhaps it is best if you look elsewhere for a wife. It is evident you cannot accept me for who I am. One thing I want you to know is I will never do anything to harm the people I love. I know nothing of the whites, but yesterday I met my white uncle while I was at the graves of my white parents. As much as I love the parents who raised me, despite the circumstances of my birth, I also want to know more about the people who gave birth to me."

"Are you saying you would choose them over us?"

"You are putting words into my mouth. I do not think the word to use is choose. At this point I have no idea what I will find. In my heart of hearts, I know my destiny is to be with the people I love. I also know there is another family who wonder what happened to my white parents. I must put their minds at ease and it is possible I will be able to bridge the gap between our two races."

Anger and perhaps betrayal flashed in Sly Coyote's eyes. Just looking at him, she knew his would not be the first rejection she would experience from the people who loved her for her entire life.

It breaks my heart to see him turn and walk away from me without saying another word. I wanted him to tell me there was no other maiden he wants to court. I wanted to hear him say I would always hold his heart. I now know Sly Coyote would only be the first among the people to turn his back on me.

~ * ~

The next morning, Sky Eyes prepared to return to the graves of her white parents with the parents she'd known and loved for her entire life. The night before, she saw her father return from the meeting with the leaders with less enthusiasm than when he left earlier in the day. That mixed with the reaction she'd received from Sly Coyote made her wonder if she would ever feel welcomed and loved in the village where she'd grown from infant to woman.

With them were her brother, Hunting Hawk, the medicine man, Angry Otter, and their chief Stalking Badger. Although she hoped the journey to meet with the white men would have been a joyous one, a cloud of doubt and suspicion hung over their party as they made their way to the designated meeting spot.

Ahead of them, she saw three of the men they had seen two days earlier. Thomas stood ahead of the other two men who bore a strong resemblance to one another. Sky Eyes thought the younger men standing behind Thomas looked terrified to see the four warriors approaching them. Even though they'd seen Running Deer and Hunting Hawk two days earlier, they had not seen them dressed in their ceremonial best as they were today.

Thomas took several steps toward them with his hand outstretched. Sky Eyes remembered him doing the same thing the first time they met and wondered if this was a standard greeting among white men. Even if it wasn't, it showed her father and the others he carried no weapons and posed no threat to them.

"I am pleased to see you have returned to meet with us. We cannot offer you the comfort of a lodge for our meeting but we went hunting yesterday and we can offer you some meat we have roasted in your honor."

Sky Eyes glanced at Angry Otter and saw the acceptance of what Thomas told them. He was following the rules of the people in offering guests food to sustain them.

"We accept your hospitality. As for a lodge for our meeting, it is unnecessary. We are comfortable seating ourselves around your fire."

Once they were seated, Thomas again took the lead in beginning the conversation. "When we met before, I asked you about my brother, Robert. After you left, I found the cross marking his grave with his name carved on the crosspiece. I ask you again if you knew him."

Sky Eyes held her breath, waiting for one of the men to respond. Instead, her mother answered Thomas' question.

"It was fourteen springs ago when I gave birth to twins, a boy and a girl. The girl lived only a matter of days. While I was grieving her loss, Running Deer and I came to the creek to search for spring herbs and vegetables. As we searched, I heard the cries of a newborn baby. I found a woman who was dying of childbirth fever in a white man's cabin. She told me her husband, Robert, had been killed in an accident and she knew she was dying. She wanted us to bury her next to him. She told us her name was Martha and asked me to take her daughter, Kathryn, and raise her as my own."

Sky Eyes looked at Thomas and saw him wiping unmanly tears from his eyes. It was evident the man was grieving for the brother and sister-in-law he had lost so many years earlier without even knowing of their deaths.

"Since I had lost my daughter and had more than enough milk, to say nothing of love for the child who was soon to lose her natural mother, it only made sense to take her to our village. Over these many turnings of the seasons, I have thought of her in no way other than my daughter, Sky Eyes."

"Has she been treated differently because of her white blood?" Thomas asked.

This time it was Angry Otter who answered Thomas' question. "Those of us who are the elders in the village remember the day when Morning Star returned with her white daughter. Among our people children are cherished whether they are of our race or are white. She has become a good woman and although over the years we have overlooked her white blood, those of our people who are younger are skeptical of where her loyalties lie. What are your intentions concerning Kathryn?"

Hearing Angry Otter call her by her white name made Sky Eyes realize it was entirely possible she would no longer be welcome among the people she'd known for her entire life.

She looked to her white uncle to see his reaction to the words of Angry Otter.

"My brother, Robert, and I were very close as I am certain Kathryn is close to everyone in her family. I grieve the loss of my brother and his wife. That said, I now say prayers of thanksgiving that your people gave his daughter a good life. I can tell she has been raised with love and taught respect. I am anxious to be in contact with my family. It is past the time when they should be told of the fate of my brother and his wife as well as to tell them of the daughter who survived when she should have died without her parents. As much as I want to get to know her, I have no home. We are exploring your lands not to take them from you, but to live in harmony with you. If we are able to live as good neighbors with your people, I would feel it a privilege to get to know my niece."

Angry Otter remained quiet for a moment then nodded to Stalking Badger.

"I am Stalking Badger," he began. "I am the chief of these people. We have been in council ever since Running Deer told us of your presence on the land. If you know anything about our people, you must realize the land is not ours to claim or keep anyone else from claiming. We have heard of the coming of your people to this land. We also know it is nothing we can stop. What we ask of you is that you be good neighbors and allow us to hunt as we have hunted since the beginning of time. We also ask you to take Sky Eyes with you and teach her the ways of the whites. For her to remain in our midst would put our people in danger."

"Danger?" Sky Eyes echoed unable to keep her silence any longer. "I have never been a danger to anyone. Before these men came I had no idea of my white blood."

"Hear Stalking Badger out, daughter," Running Deer said. "The danger would not come from you. The council has agreed the danger would come from the white men who would see you as white and come to steal you away from us. Should that happen, the men of our village would defend you with their lives, bringing bloodshed and death to our people. It is best if you are with your white uncle where you could learn the ways of your white parents. With you living with your white uncle you would still be close to those of us who have raised and loved you without reservation."

The memory of Sly Coyote's rejection entered Sky Eyes' mind. No matter what her father said, the leaders were rejecting her just as Sly Coyote did less than a complete day earlier.

"I have no desire to endanger the people. For the second time in the past day I have felt the rejection of those I thought loved me. As much as I love my family, I understand why I am no longer welcomed by the people. I only ask you bring me any possessions you deem to be mine. If there is nothing you consider as such, I will understand. I am certain I will be able to make new things."

In frustration, she turned her back on her family and walked the short distance to her white uncle.

"I will be honored to come with you. I promise I will not be a burden to you. I will learn your language as well as your ways. I pray the people will allow us to build a lodge close to the graves of my white parents."

"No," Morning Star screamed. "You cannot send my daughter away from me."

"It is for the best, Mother," Sky Eyes said, hurrying to her mother's side. "Last night Sly Coyote rejected me because of my white blood. He is only the first of many who will turn against me. If my white uncle is allowed to build a lodge close to the graves of my white parents, I will never be far away from you. I am certain you will always be welcome in whatever lodge I call home."

Without further conversation with the people she'd known all her life, Sky Eyes went to stand with the strangers who were now her people.

"Are you sure this is what you want to do?" Thomas asked.

"The people have given me no other option. I pray you will treat me fairly and not beat me when I do not learn your ways as quickly as you think I should."

"I would never beat you. I will treat you as I would my own daughter. Family is too important to me to ever return love with cruelty."

Sky Eyes turned to get a final glimpse of her people returning to the village. Never again would she be called Sky Eyes. From this day forward she would be Kathryn, even though the name was hard to pronounce and foreign upon her lips.

~ * ~

Kathryn's anger kept the tears she wanted to shed at bay. How could the people who had taken her in as an infant turn from her? Did they not know she loved each and every one of them? She doubted it. In a matter of two days they had turned their backs on her. She now had a hole in her heart she doubted would ever heal.

She felt Thomas embrace her. "I am so sorry for what has happened today."

"It is what I expected. Yesterday, the man I was planning to marry told me he wanted nothing more to do with me. The people fear the unknown and the white people are those they fear. Will you teach me your language and your customs?"

"You know I will. You are the only child of my twin brother. It was because of Robert I came to this area. I knew he came to preach the word of the Father to the natives and I envisioned him still carrying out his calling. It is by the grace of God you were found and given a loving home. I am grateful for all your adoptive parents have done for you."

"I know nothing of the white man and woman who gave me life. It was only in the spring when my mother told me the story of the death of the woman she called Martha. Since then I have seen them only in my dreams. It is not hard to believe you and my white father are brothers and now you tell me you are twins. Morning Star had twins but her daughter died on the morning she found me. I was raised to believe I was the twin sister of Hunting Hawk. I am very confused and must depend upon you because I no longer have a family to return to. I am an outcast among my people."

Sky Eyes

Tears ran down Kathryn's cheeks and for the first time in her life she shed them without shame.

~ * ~

"What are you going to do with the girl, Thomas?" Marcus asked. "I mean, she can't stay with us, can she?"

"Remember the grave marker we found yesterday? I told you it belonged to my brother, Robert. I now know his wife, Martha, lies beside him even though her grave is unmarked. The girl is their only child. She was saved from certain death by the man and woman who brought her to us today."

"You mean she's been raised by those savages? How do you know she won't murder us in our sleep? Ain't that what them savages do?"

If the situation hadn't been so serious, Thomas might have laughed at Marcus' question. "My brother contended these people were far from savages. It was his intent to teach them about Our Lord. I laughed at him when he became a missionary. I told him it was no vocation for a man. He told me it was a calling from God. For many years, I have longed to meet him again and beg his forgiveness. Now I must care for his daughter as if she were my own. I know you understood nothing of what her people were telling us, but because of her white blood, they have disowned her. She has nowhere to go. Would you have me leave her here, alone and afraid, in this wilderness to die by being attacked by one of the wild animals we have heard prowling around our campsite at night?"

Markus hung his head. "Where will you take her?"

"I left my wife and children in the home I built for them close to the great lake to the East of here. I will take her home with me and over the coming winter we will teach her the way of her white family. I will also teach her to speak English. It will be with great pleasure that I will write to my parents in New York State. They deserve to know the fate of my brother as well as the joy of having a granddaughter they never knew."

~ * ~

Katheryn sensed Hunting Hawk's arrival before she saw him enter the clearing where her white parents were buried.

"My parents sent me with your belongings," he greeted her.

"Our parents," she corrected.

"Our chief had told us you are no longer one with the people. For me you will always be my sister. I will never forget my love for you."

Katheryn looked at the small bundle Hunting Hawk carried. There were so few belongings to signify her entirety of her life. As she looked through her belongings, she noticed a change of clothing along with a bowl for eating and a knife to aid her in cooking. The knife was hidden in the folds of the garment making her believe her mother had given it to her in secret. She saw only a glimpse of the blade, immediately returning it to its hiding place in the folds of her dress. It would not do to have her brother see the one item she knew should be forbidden to her in exile from the people.

"I will also cherish the childhood memories we shared. We are both embarking on new lives. Soon you will be old enough to court one of the maidens in the village and I will be meeting the white family who left me so abruptly when my white parents lost their lives. I know the Great Spirit meant for all of this to happen to both of us. Make our parents proud of you as you grow from child to warrior and hunter."

Hunting Hawk turned from her abruptly. She understood it was because of the tears she knew he didn't want to shed in front of her. Men in their village did not cry nor did they show emotions to anyone. She was glad they were able to share this last private moment, for in the future it was clear their paths would never cross again.

She stood and watched until Hunting Hawk disappeared into the dense forest bordering, not only this clearing, but also the village she'd thought of as home for all her life. Once he was no longer in sight, she turned to the white uncle who now promised her a life in the white world.

"Are you ready to leave, Kathryn?"

Sky Eyes

The name sounded alien and yet familiar to her. "It is best if we leave here before it gets any later. The sun is already high and since I do not know how far it is to your camp, we do not want to be traveling once the sun goes down."

Thomas nodded his approval of her answer and turned toward the others in his party. He said something to them in his language. From the expression on their faces she knew they were more than ready to return to their camp. This was a place where they'd witnessed Thomas' sorrow at finding the grave of his twin brother. It was also the place where a maiden was forced from her people to go to a life she knew nothing about. She too wanted to be away from here. She hoped to put a great distance between herself and the people she considered family almost since the day of her birth. They were as dead to her as she was to them.

~ * ~

Lukas looked across the fire at the young girl who sat apart from them. She was indeed young, perhaps no more than thirteen or fourteen, but beneath the buckskin dress he could see the outline of a woman's body.

He continued to wonder how she would survive in a world of strange people who all spoke a language she could not understand.

From what Thomas said, her Christian name was Kathryn, but he interpreted the name the Indians called her as Sky Eyes. It was no wonder they'd called her that. She had the bluest eyes he'd ever seen.

He wished, like Thomas, he could speak the language of the people who raised her, but he hadn't taken the time to learn it. At the time they started their journey west, he was more interested in the promised adventure than learning to communicate with the savages. Now he saw things differently. Kathryn was certainly not a savage and neither was the woman she called mother. The father and brother were another subject. He could tell by their looks they could both be fierce warriors.

"What will happen to her now?" Lukas asked. He was hardly aware of putting voice to the question plaguing his mind.

"Shh, she'll hear you," Marcus cautioned.

"There's no need to worry," Thomas was quick to explain. "Kathryn doesn't speak English. I will take her to my family. Leona will be pleased to have an extra pair of hands to help with the children. It won't be long before she will learn both our language and our ways."

Lukas tried to envision Kathryn wearing one of the gingham dresses like the other women in the settlement, but could only think of the beautiful buckskin dress she wore with the knee-high moccasins gracing her feet.

He wondered about how the women of the settlement would accept Kathryn. Her beauty far surpassed the others and he feared their jealousy of her.

Seth Winters returned to the camp with fresh game. He hadn't accompanied them when they went to meet with the Indians. Instead, he decided to go hunting.

It surprised Lukas to see Kathryn get to her feet and take the brace of rabbits from his hands. If he was surprised to see the beautiful maiden in their midst, he was adept at hiding his emotions.

Rather than focusing on Seth, Lukas watched as Kathryn deftly skinned the animals and prepared the meat to put onto the spit so they could cook over the fire.

He thought of how much he disliked skinning and dressing game to ready it to be cooked. As the youngest member of the party the cooking duties had fallen to him. Even though he was a good marksman, the hunting had fallen to the more experienced men.

While the meat cooked, Lukas listened as Thomas spoke to Kathryn in her language. After speaking a word in native tongue, he said, "Rabbit."

Immediately, Kathryn repeated the word. The sound of her speaking in heavily accented English, made Lukas' heart leap in anticipation of the day when he would be able to carry on an intelligent conversation with her.

"You look absolutely smitten, Brother," Markus said. "Don't tell me you're falling in love with Thomas' Indian Princess."

"What if I am? She's a beautiful woman who has lived her entire life with savages. I look forward to the day when she learns to speak our language and I learn to speak hers. Just think of the conversations we could have."

"What about Suellen Nelson? I thought you were smitten with her."

"I was, but we have been gone from New York for many months. I'm not the only man who courted her. By now it is possible she's married and already breeding. I never expected her to wait for me. After meeting Kathryn, I am glad I told her to go on with her life without me, as I might not return. Face it, none of us were promised a safe return when we left New York."

Markus made no reply, giving Lukas a moment to think about Suellen. She had been the most beautiful woman he'd ever seen until he met Kathryn. She'd immediately captured not only his heart but also all of his conscious thoughts.

He knew once he went east to bring other members of their families to this land they called Wisconsin, and the community Thomas helped to establish close to the graves of his brother and sister-in-law, there would be other men who would see Kathryn's beauty.

It would be a long trip and would, more than likely, take more than two years to complete. In that time, Kathryn could possibly meet and marry another man. Even so, Lukas knew he'd have to take the chance. She was much too young for her to even consider linking her life to any man.

~ * ~

On the journey back to the established settlement, Lukas was amazed at how quickly Kathryn learned to speak the English language. Lukas listened carefully and memorized the words of her native language. It didn't take long until he participated in Kathryn's education. To say he was excited about his new-found knowledge, was an understatement. He looked forward to the time he spent in Kathryn's company each day.

CHAPTER FIVE

After a hard winter, Lukas and Markus left for New York in order to bring news to their families and lead a party of new settlers to the rich farmland they'd discovered.

Leaving Kathryn was one of the hardest things he'd ever had to do. Throughout the winter, he'd come to know her, but unlike when he left Suellen, he'd made no promises of his return. Having made the trip two years earlier, he knew the dangers he might encounter.

While the eastern tribes were relatively peaceful, there were many miles of uncivilized country for them to traverse. Anything could happen, ranging from hostilities with the natives to attacks from wild animals.

To Lukas' surprise, the trip that seemed to drag on forever when they made it two years earlier with the settlers, was finished in less than two months.

Among the families looking for news of their loved ones were Thomas' parents and sister, as well as their own parents and siblings.

"We didn't think we'd see any of you again," Thomas' father greeted them. "Tell us you have found Robert and Martha and their family. I am anxious to hear of how he has been ministering to the Indians. We're also anxious for news of Thomas and Leona as well as their family."

Lukas exchanged a knowing glance with his brother. When Markus made no move to answer the question, Lukas cleared his throat. "Thomas, Leona and the children are doing well. When we left, we learned there would be another child born in the fall. As for Robert and Martha, we found a grave with a small cross. We could barely make out the markings, but could see it was where Robert rested. While we were at the site, we met an Indian woman and her daughter. The woman told us how she came to Robert and Martha's cabin when she heard a baby crying. Once there, she found Martha was dying of childbirth fever. Martha begged the woman to take her baby and raise her as her own. She told them the baby's name was Kathryn, but they named her Sky Eyes. I must say the name suits her perfectly."

"We have a granddaughter?" Thomas' mother said. Despite her grief over the loss of her son and his wife, she seemed very interested in the existence of a granddaughter. "Is she still with the Indians? If so, will they allow us to meet her?"

In his mind's eye, Lukas could see Kathryn's Indian parents bringing her to their camp. He remembered the look of horror in her eyes at being banished from the only family she'd ever known.

"The Indians brought her to us," Marcus said, taking over the narrative. "It seems they no longer wanted her within their midst. She was white, even though she'd been raised as one of them. We were blessed when Kathryn came back to the settlement with us. You will find her to be a delightful young lady."

Lukas allowed Markus to continue explaining things to the Clay family and went in search of his oldest brother, Johnathan.

News of their arrival had spread through the small town they once called home. He was met by his sister, Mary, his brother Matthew, and his parents, but his older brother was nowhere in sight.

"Where is Johnathan?" he asked as soon as he was reunited with his parents.

"There was a great sickness in the settlement," his father began. "We lost not only Johnathan and his wife, but also their children. Mary also lost a child as did Matthew, who lost his wife. He was blessed to be able to find another with which to share his life. Suellen Harris lost her husband and it was only natural for them to be together. They each had children who needed love and guidance of two parents. The arrangement has worked out well and they are now expecting their own child."

The news that the woman he'd courted not only married a man he once considered his friend but was now the wife of his brother hit him hard. As much as he said he thought she would more than likely continue on with her life, he never expected her to marry one of his best friends, Zack Harris, let alone lose him and turn to Matthew. He would try to be happy for them, but the realization her life had gone on, brought to mind the fact Kathryn could also be married by the time he returned to Wisconsin.

~ * ~

As much as everyone wanted to begin the trip to Wisconsin territory, they all knew there was much preparation to do before they would be able to leave.

Since Marcus and Lukas made the journey two years earlier and back again this past spring, they had much knowledge to impart to the families who would be making the journey the following spring.

Lukas was to be spending the next months with his parents, while Marcus proposed to Emma Roberts. The engagement wasn't very long, as they were married before the geese flew south for the winter. Since Johnathan's house was now vacant, they decided to live there until it was time for them to make the trip west.

By living with his parents, Lukas often saw Matthew and Suellen. Their happiness saddened him more than he wanted to admit. She was his first love and it was hard to see her with his brother. He was so torn, but thinking about Kathryn lessened his heartache. He prayed she would be waiting for him when he returned to Wisconsin, but knew it was possible she, like Suellen would have married someone else.

CHAPTER SIX

Kathryn Clay swept the floor of the cabin she shared with her Uncle Thomas, Aunt Leona and their children. It hardly seemed possible that just one year ago, her home had been a lodge in an Indian village far to the west from where she now lived. At the time, the white man's language was as foreign to her as her language was to anyone other than her Uncle Thomas and Lucas.

She thought about how hard Lukas Palmer worked to master her language so he could help her with her studies of English. They'd spent many hours together, each speaking the other's language. She'd enjoyed their time together, even knowing with the coming spring he would be going east to bring more families to the new farms and town Thomas was working to establish.

"Why don't you sit down and rest for a while?" Leona asked, breaking into Kathryn's memory of the young man with whom she'd spent so many happy hours.

By the way her aunt held her back, Kathryn realized her child would be born soon. Although she'd only lived with her aunt and uncle for a year, she knew her aunt was having problems with this pregnancy. Unlike the five previous ones, which she told Kathryn were very easy, this time she seemed to be extremely tired. It was entirely possible Leona was getting too old to carry babies and have them born healthy.

"I don't think I'm the one who needs to rest, Aunt Leona. You look very tired. I am certain the birth of your child is near."

Leona gave her a weak smile. "You are very perceptive. I have been in labor since early this morning. I think it is time for you to go to the cabin of the midwife. I'm sure this baby will be born before nightfall. When you go, will you take the children to Erma's cabin so they will not be here when the child is born?"

Kathryn helped her aunt change her dress for a nightdress. Before getting her settled in the bed she shared with Thomas when he was home, Kathryn spread a deer hide over the top of the bed so the birth wouldn't soil the bedding. Once assured of her aunt's comfort, she gathered her young cousins to her and took them next door before going for Amy Totton, the midwife.

By the time they returned, Leona was screaming from the pains that must have become stronger while Kathryn was gone.

Even though she'd been trained to assist the women of the people when they gave birth, the midwife pushed her out of the way. Everyone in the village knew of her background and like the people who raised her, they were skeptical of what she might do to them.

Another scream came from the area where Leona labored.

"Do you know anything about being a midwife, girl?" Amy called.

"Yes Ma'am, I do. What can I do to help?"

"The baby is crosswise of the birth canal. I need to get it turned but someone must hold the light for me. I'm hoping I can do this alone. I've never had to do it before."

Kathryn assessed the woman who was only a few years older than herself. "I've done it. My native mother was a healer and a midwife. If you can hold the light, I can turn the baby."

"But-but you're..."

"I was raised by a loving family. The people who raised me lived in peace with each other and nature. I assure you I mean my aunt no harm. I only want to help her and her unborn child. If what you say is true, the child will not be born and my aunt could lose her life. Will you allow me to do what I know how to do or will you try something you've never done?"

She knew the words sounded harsh, but if the babe was blocking the birth canal, both mother and child could be dead in a matter of hours.

Although Amy looked terrified at the prospect of Kathryn delivering this child, she nodded her head and held the lantern.

Kathryn settled herself on the stool between Leona's legs and reached inside her aunt's body. She indeed found the child turned. It took all her will and strength to turn the child. Once she did, the baby followed the path of the now unblocked birth canal and slid easily from its mother's body. To Kathryn's horror, the cord was wrapped around the child's neck. Deftly, she unwrapped the constricting cord and immediately the little boy began to scream his protests at leaving his mother's womb.

She took the child to the kitchen where water heated on the stove so she could bathe the screaming little boy and rid him of the reminders of being tucked inside his mother's body.

After wrapping him in a blanket, she returned to the room where Amy cared for Leona. As soon as she stood by the bed, she knew something was terribly wrong.

"I don't know if she is going to survive this birth," Amy said. "I knew this pregnancy was going to be hard on her. After the last baby, I told her it was unwise to do this again, but she wouldn't listen to me. She has lost a lot of blood. I don't think she will be able to nurse the child. I know of a woman close by who has a child, I'm hoping she has enough milk for this little one. Can you care for your aunt while I go to this woman?"

"Of course I can. Do you know what is causing this?"

"It's the loss of blood. I'm afraid she's lost too much."

Amy hurried out of the room, while Kathryn soothed the baby and tried to remember things her mother told her about blood loss during birthing of a baby. In her mind, she could hear her mother tell her of the correct herbs to use. Throughout the spring, she had often gone out to gather the things she needed and store them in her room in the loft. She was certain she had the right combinations of medications to help her aunt.

As soon as Amy returned with Jane Oliver, Kathryn knew her presence was no longer wanted. Relieved, she hurried to her room and retrieved the proper herbs to brew into a tea for Leona to drink. Not only would it strengthen her aunt, it would also stench the flow of blood coming from her body. With the water already heating on the stove it didn't take long for the tea to steep.

By the time Kathryn returned to Leona's bedside, Amy, Jane, and the child were gone.

"Why did they take my baby from me, Kathryn? Am I going to die? I'm so frightened."

"I know how frightened you must be, Aunt Leona. You will not die. I promise. I know exactly what to do. You've lost a lot of blood and Amy was afraid you wouldn't be able to nurse the baby, so she brought Jane Oliver over to give nourishment to your son. I've told you how my mother was a healer and a midwife. I remembered what she used to give young mothers who lost too much blood during childbirth. Although I've said nothing about it, during the spring I searched for the plants I would need should anyone in the family become sick. I have brewed you a tea that should help to stop the blood flow and return your strength. Do you trust me enough to drink it?"

Leona nodded her head and with Kathryn's assistance she was able to move to a sitting position. Once she drank the tea, Kathryn went back to the kitchen for more hot water. She'd been appalled when she saw how Amy left her aunt. None of the blood from the birthing had been cleaned from her body and lying in a pool of her own blood had to be far from comfortable.

"What are you doing now?" Leona asked weakly.

"I am finishing what Amy left undone. You will feel much better once I have cleaned you up and changed your bedclothes. It is a good thing we spread the deer skin on the bed so that is not ruined."

Deftly, Kathryn changed the bedclothes as well as taking off Leona's soiled night dress. Once her aunt was naked, she began to wash the blood from Leona's legs and lower body. Her aunt murmured her thanks as she drifted off into a healing sleep.

Kathryn finished cleaning her aunt's body and getting the room back to normal when she heard the front door open. Getting up to see who was coming into the cabin, she came face to face with her uncle.

"I just saw Amy Totton as well as Jane Oliver and Erma. They told me you saved my son, but killed my wife. What happened here?"

"Amy called me to help with the birth as the child was crosswise of the birth canal. I was able to turn the child and guide him out of his mother's body. When I returned to the room, Amy told me she was going to get Jane to come and nurse the child as she was certain Aunt Leona would soon die from loss of blood."

"Did she die?"

"She did not. My mother was a healer and a midwife. I knew the proper herbs to brew a tea that would stop the blood and help her to regain her strength. Once she drank it and went to sleep, I finished the job Amy only started. I cleaned Leona's body as well as her bed and her nightdress. When I heard you come into the house, I left her sleeping peacefully. It will take a few days, but she should be better soon. Now that you are here, I will go to Erma's and bring the children back. They must be frightened by all the gossip they must be hearing."

"I am so sorry Kathryn. I should know better than to listen to the idle chatter of the women who are our neighbors. I will go and fetch the children. It is best if you are here with Leona in case she should need you."

Kathryn agreed and brewed another pot of tea before returning to Leona's beside. Although she couldn't completely understand the white man's words she could understand enough to know the women she once considered friends didn't approve of the way she was brought up and feared her presence among them. If Leona would have died today she knew the women would blame her since she was the one to turn the baby into position and help him to be born.

"I knew you would be with me when I awakened," Leona said. "Can you tell me what happened? Did I lose my baby? Am I going to die?"

Kathryn assured her aunt the baby was being cared for and she was not going to die, before she went on to explain the details of the birth.

"How did you know what to do? I know your mother was a midwife, but if Amy didn't know how to help the baby to be born how is it that you have such knowledge?"

"When I was still with the people, we had a young woman who was having trouble giving birth. Mother and I were in the midwives' lodge and she was busy with another woman who was giving birth. She couldn't help both and she told me what needed to be done. Both children and their mothers lived and when I left were healthy and happy. The same will be said of you once these first few days are over. I have just brewed some fresh tea. I want you to take it so you can regain your strength."

"When can I see my baby?"

"I will have Uncle Thomas bring him to you once he returns with the other children. I know Amy said you wouldn't be able to nurse your son, but when I changed your night dress I checked your breasts. They are full of milk and long to have your little one suckling at them. Everything will be just fine."

Leona obediently drank the tea Kathryn offered but this time did not go back to sleep. Instead, she insisted on being propped up with pillows so she would be ready to greet her husband, children and new son.

~ * ~

"Are you going to rid yourself of that savage, Thomas?" Amy asked when he arrived at Erma's cabin.

"What savage are you speaking of, Amy?" He knew he was trying hard to be civil.

"Your so-called niece, Kathryn. What she did to your wife was absolutely brutal. I have never heard of anyone reaching inside a woman's body to bring forth a child before."

"Just what would have happened if Kathryn hadn't turned the child so he could have been born?"

"Both the mother and the child would have died. Perhaps that would be for the best. What kind of a life will the child have if he is raised without a mother? I am certain she has died from the loss of blood by now. You have only Kathryn to blame for the child to be deprived of his mother and you to be deprived of your wife."

"Kathryn assures me Leona will survive this. She also told me how you left my wife lying in her own blood. Is that how you treat the other women and babies in this village? If so, I think it might be time for everyone to think about finding a new midwife. Now, Erma, I have come for my children. My wife needs them with her. Next, I will be going to Jane's cabin to get my new son. He needs to bond with his mother."

"Don't you know he will starve? I am sure even if Leona does survive she will have no milk to nourish the child."

"That will be seen. I'm certain if Leona is, as you say, unable to nurse the child, Jane will be more than happy to suckle our son as well as her own. She is a good woman and since she was willing to help out in our time of need, she will again come forward if it is necessary. In the meantime, Leona must be frantic as to where her child has been taken. I will see both of you are repaid for what you have done for my family today."

Thomas went out to the backyard where the children were playing and told them to go home to their mother. Once they were on their way, he made his way to the Oliver cabin.

As soon as he entered, he saw the child sleeping peacefully in a cradle. "I've come for my son."

"Oh, Thomas, are you certain? I heard of Leona's passing. How can you hope to take care of a newborn all by yourself?"

"I think you have things wrong. To begin with, Leona is very much alive and even if she had passed, I'm sure between Kathryn and myself we can care of my son. I thank you for your help and will repay you for your kindness."

Carefully, he lifted the baby from the cradle and opened the blanket to assess his son. He was a big baby, bigger than any of the other children they'd had before. It was no wonder the birth had been a difficult one. Other than being bigger, he was perfectly formed in every way.

"Welcome to the world, little one. As your mother and I talked about, you will be named Robert, after the brother I loved and lost."

The baby began to cry and Jane came to take the child from him. "He is hungry. I will feed him and when he is done, I will return him to your home. Go now and be with your wife and children. They need you more than this little one does."

Thomas agreed and left the cabin to return to his home. He trusted Jane and Erma more than he ever had Amy.

~ * ~

"Where is the baby?" Kathryn asked as soon as Thomas came into the cabin.

"He was hungry and Jane said she'd feed him before she brought him home."

Kathryn's heart sank. She prayed the older woman would return the baby safely, but after the way Amy treated Leona, to say nothing of the gossip she was spreading, she had her doubts. "Leona will be disappointed. She was looking forward to nursing her child. She's also looking forward to seeing you. I told the children she would want to see you before she saw them. I sent them to wash up for supper. There is a stew cooking so you will all have a nourishing supper."

"Of course, I'll go in and see Leona immediately. I allowed my anger over the gossip Amy is spreading drive thoughts of seeing my wife from my mind. I am certain once her lies come to light, as well as what you did to save both Leona's and Robert's lives, her services will no longer be needed. It's entirely possible people will want you to take over her duties. Are you ready for such responsibilities?"

Kathryn was astounded. She only did what she'd learned to do from her mother, but she never thought the whites would want her to help their women birth their babies. "I would be honored, but I doubt many of the people would be comfortable with me attending their wives and unborn children."

Thomas didn't answer her. Instead he headed toward the room where Leona waited for her child to be brought to her. Turning her attention to the stew, she let her mind wander to what Thomas said earlier.

She'd been shocked when her uncle named the child for her white father and even more so when he suggested she become the midwife for the women in this area. If she thought there was hatred for her from Amy before, she knew it would be doubled now.

A knock at the cabin door interrupted her thoughts. Drying her hands on the towel she used to dry the dishes, she hurried to answer it. To her relief, Jane stood at the door holding the baby in her arms.

"He's been fed and burped. Now he's ready for a nap. How is Leona doing?"

"She's weak from the loss of blood, but I know holding her son will be the best medicine she could get."

Jane handed the child to Kathryn. "I'm sorry I didn't bring him back sooner, but Amy told me Leona had died. I knew I shouldn't listen to her gossip but so much was happening so quickly I believed her. Thomas told me you saved the baby's life and you are also treating Leona. My sister, Mary, is having a child soon. When she does, would you come and help with the birth?"

Kathryn knew her mouth hung open, but Jane's request took her completely by surprise. "I would be honored but wouldn't that endanger your friendship with Amy?"

"I honestly don't have a friendship with her. After my last baby was born, I told my man I would have him take me to my mother's house if I were to have another baby. Amy was very rough with me when she delivered the child, but my husband told me it was only my imagination. He is friends with Amy's husband. I told him I don't care about who he is friends with, but I didn't want to have to deal with Amy again."

"Thank you for your kind words, Jane. I appreciate your friendship."

Once Jane left, Kathryn took the sleeping baby to his mother. Leona's eyes immediately brightened when she saw the child who had been taken away so quickly after his birth.

"He is a handsome boy," Thomas said as he gazed lovingly at both his wife and his new son. "I have named him Robert, for my brother, as we talked about."

"It is a perfect name, just as he is a perfect child. Kathryn says I will be able to allow him to suckle and he will get enough nourishment, but I fear I have not enough strength to care for everyone I love."

"Do not concern yourself with that," Kathryn assured her. "I will be happy to care for the house and the children."

"Now that my work on the new farm as well as the town is finished for the winter, I will be able to help Kathryn." Thomas turned his gaze from his wife to his niece.

"I doubt I will need much help, Uncle Thomas. Had I not come with you, I would have been married with children of my own. Your children are so well behaved I know I will have no problem. My only fear is that I will not be able to help them with their schooling."

"Don't worry about that," Thomas assured her. "I will be here to help the children and I will continue your lessons. I am so pleased to think you are learning to read and write when just a year ago, you couldn't speak our language."

Kathryn thought about everything she'd learned over the past year. Although she pronounced several of the words of her white parents' language strangely, she did understand almost everything people said to her. She also enjoyed learning to read the words she was now speaking and being able to write her name and cypher simple sums.

~ * ~

Fall turned to winter and the entire family began packing their belongings for the trip to the farms and settlement close to the village where Kathryn had grown from dependent infant to independent woman.

The thought of being so close to the people was comforting and yet bothered her. She knew they wouldn't recognize Kathryn as being Sky Eyes who had spent most of her life in their midst. She was also aware of the fact she would not be welcomed in their lodges.

Although Leona was now able to do simple tasks around the house, her strength was slow in returning. It made Kathryn wonder what would have happened if she had not been able to stop the flow of blood caused by Robert's birth. Amy took the baby and ran from the cabin leaving Leona to die.

When it was time for Mary's baby to be born, it was Kathryn who had been summoned to the birthing bed. It was no secret Amy was not happy with what Kathryn did for the first-time mother and her baby.

Thomas was sitting at the table enjoying his morning tea when there was a knock at the door. He got up from the table to answer it.

"What are you going to do about that savage living in your house?" Amy asked without even a proper greeting.

"If you're speaking of my niece, Kathryn, I am doing nothing. She not only saved the life of my son but that of my wife."

"I would hardly say that. I attended the birth. She shouldn't have interfered."

"If she had not interfered, as you say, my wife would have labored longer than necessary with the child unable to be born because of his position. Also, if she had not interfered, Leona's loss of blood would have killed her. Kathryn was able to staunch the flow and give Leona a tea that helped her regain her strength. As I recall, it was you who took my son away when my wife was able to allow him to suckle. The way I see it you have done more harm than good."

Anger radiated from Amy's eyes. "I've been told when Mary Anders gave birth, it was that savage they called to be the midwife. I am the midwife in this area and people would be wise not to forget it."

"You will not have to worry about such things in the future, as I know of no women who are breeding at this time. By next summer we will be gone and not have to listen to your rants. I am pleased to think your man decided to stay here and not go with us to the unknown."

Without giving Amy time to respond to what he just said, Thomas shut and barred the door.

"Good riddance," he said as he turned to Kathryn, who was shaping loaves of bread to be baked as soon as they had risen. "I feel sorry for the women who will continue to be at her mercy while in the birthing bed."

"You are too harsh, Uncle. She means well and it must have bothered her when I was called to assist Mary rather than her. In her eyes, I am young and untested. She does not feel me qualified, even though I have been helping Morning Star for many years."

Thomas shook his head. "I can understand why you call your mother by her proper name but in all aspects, other than giving birth to you, she is your mother and deserves to be called by that name."

"I know you try to understand, but I doubt anyone in the white world will ever be able to relate to my life. Until the spring, before the day I met you, I had no idea I was born of white parents. Among the people, I was accepted by all who knew me. Even the thought of me being born white was forgotten as I grew up as one of them. Once it was revealed to everyone, I was no longer accepted. Even the man I was going to marry dismissed me. He wanted nothing to do with a white woman. In the blink of an eye my life changed completely. I had to watch as my parents turned their backs on me. They are no longer Mother and Father. Instead they will forever be Morning Star and Running Deer to me. My true parents are buried under the prairie grass close to where you are building your farm."

Kathryn could see the confusion in her uncle's eyes, and ached for him. She wanted to make him understand, but knew he never would.

"All that matters not to me is that I will be forever in their debt for them taking you in and raising you as though you were your own. You are a beautiful young woman, and without their love and guidance, you too would rest beneath the grass of the prairie."

Kathryn said no more on the subject. Although she was excited to be moving to Thomas and Leona's new homestead, the thought of living so close to the village where she grew up was frightening. When she first met her uncle, the chief and the elders gave their permission for the farms and town to be built but would the time that had passed change their minds? The people distrusted the whites. It was evident by the way she had been treated when her true identity was revealed.

CHAPTER SEVEN

Lukas thought the hold of winter would never end. Finally, just after the first of April, they were ready to leave for Wisconsin. He realized the trip would be much longer with the line of wagons joining them. He knew it would be August before they would reach their destination.

Over the winter there had been much discussion on who would be accompanying them on the trip. It came as a relief when no one of the Palmer family, other than Marcus and Emma, would be returning with them. Their parents' health wasn't good enough for such a long journey. Matthew and Suellen thought the sojourn would be far too arduous with their growing family. Suellen had one child from her first marriage and Matthew added two more children to the mix, to say nothing of their newborn. Meanwhile, Mary thought the adventure would be exciting, but her new husband didn't want to relocate as his farm was a prosperous one.

Thomas' parents, Ester and Ruben Clay, along with their daughter Bernadine and her husband David Meyer decided they would be headed west. With them were Leona's parents, Jacqueline and Michael Adams, as well as their son Saul and his wife Eve. Even though the number of wagons was small, they still anticipated the trip would be a long one.

Since Marcus and his wife were driving the wagon, Lukas opted to ride his horse during the trip. At night, while the newly married couple slept inside the wagon, he chose not to join them, sleeping in his blankets under the wagon.

During the days, Lukas spent his time scouting ahead on the trail while providing meat for the evening meals. On this trip, he wasn't the one dressing and preparing the meat, he was now the provider.

At night, while the families contemplated their future in the virgin territory, he studied the maps he and Markus drew on their two previous journeys through the area. On them were marked areas where hostile tribes ruled and ones to be avoided. Also noted were where the best hunting was available.

The progress they were making was remarkable. By early June they were more than half way to their destination. All Lukas could think about was each day they traveled, he was getting closer to Kathryn and he prayed she would still be waiting for him.

~ * ~

The winter seemed to be never ending but, at last, spring came to Wisconsin, as well as area around the shore of the big lake where the snow fell heavily ever since the geese flew south. With it was the hope that by the end of the summer the new settlers from the east would be arriving.

Day by day, the current residents of the settlement stayed busy packing their wagons in preparation for the move from the big lake to the prairie of waving grass. For many of the people Kathryn had come to know and respect, there were decisions to be made. Many were going with Thomas to the land far to the west but even more of them were remaining in their established homes and farms.

While the women decided what they would be taking with them, the men spent their days at the new area in the west, building homes and establishing farms.

A commotion brought people from their homes. Kathryn was awed by the line of tented wagons arriving from the south side of the lake.

The white canvas coverings made the wagons into moving homes on wheels. The concept excited Kathryn, making her anxious for her Uncle Thomas to finish their wagon so they too could leave this area for the farm being established in the west.

"Kathryn!"

She turned to see Lukas coming toward her. It had been a year ago, when he left with his older brother, Marcus, for the far away village of New York. Being the youngest he was only two years older than Kathryn. Before he left, he'd been a frequent visitor at the Thomas' home. At the time, she'd fantasied about him asking her to be his wife. The fantasies ended when he went east with his brother.

"I'm so happy to see you, Kathryn," he said as he approached her. "Has some young man stolen your heart?"

Kathryn could feel a blush creeping into her cheeks. "You know better than that, Lukas. No one here wants to be associated with a woman who was raised by Indians, or savages, as they call them."

"Good. I'm glad no one else has been captivated by your charms. I've thought of nothing other than asking Thomas if I can court you since before I left."

"I'm flattered, but do you have any idea what people will say about you?"

"They'll say I'm one lucky devil to be in love with the most beautiful woman in the territory."

Behind them many reunions were going on, including those between Thomas and his family as well as Leona and her family.

She hardly had time to ponder the answer to Lukas' question when a young woman who closely resembled Thomas approached her.

"Oh, Kathryn," the woman said as she hugged her tightly. "I can see both my brother Robert, and my sister-in-law, Martha, in you. I'm your Aunt Bernadine Meyer. Come and meet my parents, your grandparents."

Kathryn turned her attention from Lukas to the older couple standing with Thomas and Leona. The man reminded her of an older version of her Uncle Thomas while the woman closely resembled the woman who told her she was her Aunt Bernadine. They were looking at her with love in their eyes, but would they accept her after she'd been raised by people they probably considered savages? Would she ever be good enough to be the white woman she was born to be?

She allowed Bernadine to lead her toward the couple who were her grandparents. As soon as she got close to them, she could see tears in the older woman's eyes.

"I can't believe it. Your father was my first born. I would have known you were his daughter just by looking at you."

Kathryn allowed her grandmother to pull her into a loving embrace; the tears the older woman shed soaked into the bodice of Kathryn's dress convincing her they were sincere.

"Tell me girl, how did my son die?" her grandfather asked.

Kathryn broke the embrace and took a step forward toward the old man.

"I'm afraid I cannot. I was only days old when Morning Star and Running Deer found me. My mother was close to death from childbirth fever. What she told Morning Star was her husband, my father, was killed in an accident before my birth and now she was dying. She asked to be buried next to him. I have been told Running Deer wrapped her in a blanket from the bed and buried her with things he found in the cabin he felt were important to her in life. Other than that, there is nothing else I know."

"I am sorry, child. Thomas has told me the same story, but I wanted to hear it for myself. For all these years, I've wondered what happened to my son and his wife. I was devastated when they went into the wilderness and never contacted us again. I had no idea if they had children or if the savages took their lives."

Kathryn bit her lip rather than speak out. To her the people weren't savages. Until just a few years earlier they were the only family she knew. They taught her to be a hard-working woman who loved the Great Spirit. They were gentle and loving until the truth about her birth became public knowledge. It was then they turned their backs on her.

"Morning Star and Running Deer were loving parents. I was raised with my brother, Hunting Hawk. Had my parentage not been revealed, I would have been married now. Sly Coyote was to be my husband, but once he learned I was not of the people he took back his proposal. Because of my white parents, he did not want me. Because of the people who raised me, are you going to put me aside as well?"

Her outspoken words seemed to shock the older man.

"I would never put you aside. On the contrary, one day I hope to meet Morning Star and Running Deer to offer them my thanks for saving the life of my granddaughter. I still have the last letter we received from your father. He told of the cabin he'd built and the child they were looking forward to. After that there were no more letters."

"Didn't my mother send you a letter after my father's death?"

The old man shook his head, sadly. "Even though Martha could read and write, I am certain she had enough to do in keeping her home and carrying you to send us a letter. Thomas insisted something had happened to your father, but I never wanted to believe it. As your grandmother said, your father was our first born. He was also special in our lives as were all of our children."

"You will have more time to learn of Kathryn's life," Leona said. "For now, I have the midday meal prepared. Food is more important than information that can take a lifetime for you to learn everything you want to know."

Leona's interruption was a welcome distraction. Over the months of living in the white world, Kathryn learned to speak the language of her parents and along with her cousins was learning to read as well as write. Even so, she was not completely comfortable conversing with strangers. For the most part she'd kept to herself making only a few friends within the village.

With the long-awaited arrival of the wagons from the east, everyone brought food for the noon day meal. Thomas and Leona were not the only ones with families coming to join them. Some of the people would be staying in the area around the big lake while others planned to move further west with Thomas and the others.

Just outside of Thomas and Leona's cabin, long tables had been set up and groaned under the weight of all the food. Kathryn waited while others filled their plates. Earlier the children had been given their portions and told to take their seats on the grassy area on the edge of the encroaching forest.

As usual, Kathryn hovered next to the little ones keeping watch for any wild animals who might be coming from within the forest tempted by the smell of the food.

"Aren't you going to eat?"

Kathryn turned at the sound of Marcus' voice.

"I will, in time. I am not as trusting of the animals who prowl close to our homes when there is easy food available. It is best if I wait until everyone else is fed and keep an eye on the children."

"I could watch the children for you so you can get something to eat. I happen to know my brother has been looking for you."

"To be truthful, I'm not very hungry. There is too much excitement. I need time to myself to think about the future and the family who now claims me as their own. I am certain your wife is looking for you. You should go ahead and eat, I'll be along shortly."

Marcus shook his head and made his way back to where the adults were gathered, leaving Kathryn alone with her thoughts.

She heard the shouts of the children as they played games of tag as well as hide and seek. Watching them, she remembered the carefree days when she herself was a child. Memories of the children who played on the fringes of the village, always mindful of the animals lingering in the dark recesses of the forest waiting to claim one of the little ones for their evening meal.

Unbidden tears sprung to her eyes as she recalled the way she played with her brother as well as the other children in the village. She shed them, knowing she would never again be accepted in their company.

A growl from deep within the forest drew her attention away from her wayward thoughts. She immediately recognized it as belonging to one of the wolverines who populated the area. Although they probably wouldn't kill one of the children, she knew they were likely to attack and maim anyone who got into their path.

"Quickly children, we must get back to the adults and the celebration."

"But why, Aunt Kathryn?" Tommy Junior questioned.

"Did you not hear the cry of the wolverine?"

Tommy shook his head.

"Well, I did. We are in his path and it isn't safe for us to be here. Now hurry. I want you all safe."

The children obeyed and Kathryn palmed her knife just in case the wolverine wanted to follow them.

"Is something wrong?" Thomas asked, once the children were safely back within the company of the adults.

"I heard a wolverine in the forest. It was no longer safe for the children to play there. It's a good thing I decided to watch over them. I am not saying the animal would have killed any of them but I have seen the damage a wolverine can do to human flesh. I wouldn't wish such a fate upon any of these innocent little ones."

"You are a wonder, Kathryn. What would we do without you? If I'm not mistaken you haven't had anything to eat and there is a young man looking for you. Eat your fill because tomorrow morning we will be leaving for our journey to the west."

Kathryn nodded and made her way toward the tables that were still laden with food. Knowing the children were now safe, she filled a plate and made her way to one of the tables where some of the other women were waiting for her.

"Is it true you're leaving with them in the morning?" Amy asked.

"You know it's true, Amy Totton. I have always known I would be going with Uncle Thomas and Aunt Leona to their new farm. Since you aren't going, someone will have to act as midwife to the women. I'm sure you will be more than happy to have me gone so you can see to the needs of the women here without worrying about how I might interfere with your practice. I am sorry to think we couldn't be friends."

Rather than continuing her meal, Kathryn pushed aside her plate and got up from the table.

"Where are you going?" Leona questioned.

"I have packing to finish."

"I've been telling you she's nothing more than a savage with no proper manners." She heard Amy proclaim to everyone at the table.

"I have manners," Kathryn said, turning back to face the one person she saw as an enemy within the white community. "I've held my tongue ever since Robert was born, ever since you ran out of the cabin leaving Leona and Robert to die because you didn't know what to do to save them. I may have been raised by people whose skin was not white like yours. Because of things I learned from them, Leona and Robert both survived and are living healthy lives. Of course, to you I will never be good enough. It's taken me a long time to learn the language of my family so I can be understood by everyone around me. I'm sorry if my manners do not suit you but by this time tomorrow I will be on my way to Thomas and Leona's new farm and you won't have to be bothered by the likes of me."

She turned on her heel and stormed away from the women seated at the table.

"Well, there you have it, Thomas Clay," Amy shouted. "How can you allow a dirty savage like her in your home? She will murder you in your sleep once you're away from here. She'll sneak back to those savages and arrange for them to kill the whole lot of you. Mark my words, you'll regret the day you brought her to our community."

"You are speaking of my family, Amy Totten. Had not Morning Star and Running Deer come along and given my sister-in-law a proper burial, as well as taking my niece to be raised as their own, I shudder to think what could have become of her. Had she not survived, my wife and son would have died. I will thank you to keep your opinions to yourself."

Kathryn heard the entire exchange. She knew she was no longer welcome here. It had been the same when those she lived with in the village where she'd been raised had turned their backs on her. Staying in either place was no longer an option. Lukas proclaimed his love but would it last? She doubted it.

CHAPTER EIGHT

Kathryn waited until the entire household slept before making her way to the wagon Thomas packed earlier. After taking her few belongings, she quietly slipped away. From here on she would make her own way. It was possible if she went south she could find a place where no one knew of her upbringing and would welcome her as a midwife.

She took advantage of the full moon and followed the shore of the big lake to the south. By day, she found shelter in the caves lining the bluffs at the edge of the lake.

~ * ~

"Thomas, Thomas," Leona called. "Kathryn has run away. I found this note from her."

Thomas took the paper from his wife's hand. Although it was printed in a childish scrawl the meaning was plainly clear. The verbal exchange between himself and Amy had been overheard.

Without saying a word, Thomas took the paper and stormed out of the house. Outside people were loading the last of their belongings into their wagons and preparing to leave. With determination, he made his way to Amy's cabin.

Being early in the morning, he pounded on the door for several seconds before Amy finally answered.

"Why are you making such a racket so early in the morning?" she asked.

"I hope you are happy. Because of your surly behavior, Kathryn has left us. We found this note this morning. In it she says her upbringing has ruined our lives and she is better off alone. We were a happy family until your outburst yesterday afternoon."

"You can't blame me for her leaving. Blame those savages. Isn't it true they move on a whim? At least that's what I've heard. She is only doing what she was taught."

"The people who raised her have been living in the same location for generations. She has only learned hatred from you. I am pleased to think you will not be joining us, but losing Kathryn saddens me."

"What are you saying about Kathryn?" Lukas said from behind him.

Thomas turned to face the young man who only last night asked for permission to once again court his niece. "She has left, thanks to Amy's harsh words. In the note Leona found this morning, she says she doesn't want anyone to follow her."

"Do you think I'll be content to go to my new farm without her? I've thought of nothing but making her my wife the whole time I was in the east. You and the rest of them can go ahead. I'm going to find Kathryn. Do you have any idea which way she might have gone?"

Thomas shook his head. "I'd go with you, but I have a family to think of. I wish you luck. If you do find her, bring her home to the family who loves her."

~ * ~

Lukas watched as Thomas returned to his cabin. He couldn't understand why Thomas would continue on to his farm as well as their new life without searching for Kathryn. Then he did say he had a family to consider.

"Well, I don't have a family," he declared to no one but himself.

"Did you say something, brother?"

He turned to face Marcus. "Thomas just told me Kathryn has run away.

I can't believe Thomas is considering going west without her. I'm going to find her."

"I know you're taken with her, but how do you propose to find someone who doesn't want to be found?"

"That's my business. You and the rest of the people go ahead. When I find her, I'll look for the nearest preacher and make her my wife before we join you."

~ * ~

The last light of day was fading when Kathryn prepared to continue her journey to the south. Although she'd taken no food with her when she made her hasty departure, she found some edible plants in the predawn before she settled into her hiding place for the daylight hours.

She was used to enjoying the plants that grew in the countryside without having to light a fire in order to prepare them. Once she put more distance between herself and the community she just left, she would have to do some hunting. Even though she could survive on the vegetables she knew at some point she would need meat to sustain her.

The cave she found gave her adequate shelter but she didn't take the chance of lighting a fire. Instead, she used her belongings as a pillow as she made her bed on the hard ground. It had been several months since she last slept on anything other than a soft bed in her uncle's home and if the truth be known she was a bit uncomfortable at first. The sensation lasted only a few minutes before she fell into a deep sleep.

In her dreams, she was living on Thomas' new farm, but many of the other people wanted nothing to do with her because she'd been raised by the savages. Almost immediately, the dream changed to one of her returning to the people who raised her. One by one they turned their backs on the white woman who dared to return to the village of her childhood.

You are not welcome in the white community, nor are you welcome among the people. It is your destiny to spend your life alone.

The dream faded and peaceful slumber replaced it.

Outside the door, the sounds of nature greeted Kathryn when she awoke. Outside the opening of the cave, she could see the long shadows of late afternoon spreading across the beach leading to the lake just beyond her sanctuary.

Before beginning her journey, Kathryn left the security of the cave to see if anyone followed her. *I still have the instincts I was brought up learning. I know how to become one with the vegetation and watch for intruders, may they walk on two legs or four.*

Assured she was alone, she ventured out to begin her evening journey to the south. Throughout her flight away from the whites who distrusted her, she'd been careful to cover her tracks. Now as she looked out on the beach below the cave, she could see no other tracks besides those of a deer who came to drink and still lingered on the edge of the water.

She ate the last of the greens she'd gathered the night before. They would sustain her on her journey. Tonight, the moon was still almost full and the sky was clear. It made traveling easy. If she was lucky she might come upon a farm or perhaps another cave where she could spend the coming day.

Her luck held as she started out on her way. The moon played with the clouds but still the night was clear enough for her to make her way along the lake shore. She found she could stay away from the sandy beach, successfully hiding her footprints in the grassy area close to the forest.

By daybreak, she saw a farmhouse looming in front of her. She could also hear the lowing of the cows as they were driven in from the pasture for the morning milking. For a moment, she thought of retreating into the forest, but thoughts of returning to the company of other people overrode her concerns of not being accepted by the whites who lived and worked on the farm.

Her contemplations kept her attention for too long, since the farmer was now making his way toward her. There was no time for her to retreat back into the forest.

"Little Lady, what are you doing out here all alone?"

Kathryn knew she had to think quickly before she answered his question. "I'm heading south in the hopes of finding a place to settle. Since my parents have died I didn't want to continue on with the people with whom we were traveling."

"Didn't you have people you could be with?"

She certainly didn't expect such a question. "We were on our way west when there was an accident. Our wagon was destroyed and my parents died. I want to find a place where I can become a midwife. My mother trained me as she had been trained."

"Then you're in luck. There's a town not far away from here. I know they have no midwife, since when my wife birthed our last baby, there was no one but me to help her. You come with me and my Maude will fix you something to eat. You look plumb tuckered out."

Tired from her night long journey, Kathryn followed him up to the farmhouse.

"What is your name lass?" he asked before they reached the house.

"It's Kathryn Clay," she replied, immediately sorry she didn't think to call herself by a different name. She couldn't very well say her name was Sky Eyes and any other white names didn't seem to fit her.

"I'm Ruben Morgan, and as I said earlier, my wife is Maude. I'm sure she'll be pleased to have you staying with us as she's expecting our next babe very soon."

It's possible this was meant to be. If I can establish myself as a midwife by delivering the Morgan baby, I might be able to find a place where I am needed.

She didn't have time for any more thoughts as they'd reached the cabin. Maude Morgan stood in the doorway with a young child in her arms and three older children tugging at her skirt.

"We have a visitor, Maude," Ruben announced.

"I see. Do you have family with you, girl?"

"No Ma'am, it's just me. My family was killed in an accident and I'm alone in the world. I was hoping to make it to somewhere I can work as a midwife."

With her free hand, Maude caressed her bulging belly. "Looks like I might be your first patient. This babe is anxious to make it into the world. I have breakfast cooking on the stove, so when Ruben is done with the milking we can eat. You're welcome to join us and stay until at least the babe is born. I hope you don't mind sleeping in the hayloft. As you can see, this cabin is bursting at the seams."

Kathryn agreed to Maude's suggestion and immediately started to work helping with the meal that was cooking on the hearth.

As though relieved to have the extra help, Maude sat down in one of the chairs, emitting a sigh. "I won't turn down your help. Ruben didn't say, what is your name?"

"It's Kathryn, Ma'am."

"None of that Ma'am stuff. You're to call me Maude. I'm sure we're going to become good friends. Especially with this child anxious to be born. This will be my fifth child in as many years. I have to admit as much as I love each of these little ones, I wish they hadn't come so close together."

"When I have time, I'll go out looking for some herbs for you to brew into a tea that will keep you from conceiving another child until you want to."

"Is there such an herb?"

"Yes, my mother taught me all about the herbs and what they cure. As long as you drink the tea every day there will be no more babies until you are ready for them."

"If this will work the way you say, it will be a good thing. I won't think about it now, as there is too much work to do to be dwelling on what could be."

Kathryn understood what Maude meant. She also saw how tired Maude looked. "As long as I'm here, you should be able to relax. I can help with the cooking while you take things easy. Once we have everyone fed, I will check on the progress of the baby. From the looks of things, you are carrying low, so it's possible the child has dropped into position."

CHAPTER NINE

Unable to decide in which direction Kathryn might have gone, Lukas took one of the saddle horses to go in search of her. He considered heading toward the west where the others were going, but realized if she wanted to get away from the whites who chased her away with their harsh words, she wouldn't go to the place where they were heading.

Knowing the lake stood to the east he had to choose, north or south. On a hunch, he turned his horse to the north. Considering her Indian family and friends turned their backs on her, she wouldn't go back to them. They, like the white community, must terrify her. It was possible she was trying to do things on her own.

Staying close to the shoreline of the lake, he searched in vain for any sight of a trail left by Kathryn as she ran away from the people she now considered her enemy.

By evening, he found a cave, and once he was certain no animal inhabited it he bedded down for the night. He was hopeful by morning he would be able to overcome Kathryn. How far could she have gotten on foot with no horse?

~ * ~

Kathryn found the hayloft of the barn on the Morton property to be very comfortable. Maude insisted on giving her blankets as well as a feather pillow.

During the day, she enjoyed helping Maude with the children and the household chores. After breakfast each morning, Kathryn took the children to the forest in search of herbs and edible greens. As she did, she told them the stories of the plants and animals she'd learned from her mother as a young child.

"How do you know so much?" Maude and Ruben's oldest, Abraham, asked.

"I just know the things my mother taught me."

"You said your mother was dead."

Kathryn thought about the half-truth she'd been caught in. In reality, Morning Star was as dead to her as her true mother, Martha.

"Maude, is Kathryn with you?" Ruben called, his voice sounding as though he was out of breath.

"Yes, we are right here. Is something wrong?"

"Edwin Peters' wife, Caroline, is giving birth and as you know there's no midwife in the village. He hoped you could come and help him since he doesn't know what to do."

Kathryn watched as Maude put her hand to her back. "I'm close to my own delivery. I doubt I could walk that far. Is it possible you could go, Kathryn?"

Without hesitation, Kathryn handed her herb basket to one of the children and hurried to Ruben's side. "I must go to the loft and get my herbs. Once I do, I will be ready to go and help Caroline Peters."

"Herbs?" Ruben questioned.

"Healing herbs I've been collecting throughout the summer and even more since I have been with you. They grow here in abundance and I've been fortunate enough to find them and allow them to dry in the barn."

Without further comment, Ruben waited as Kathryn gathered her packets of healing herbs. Once she returned to the dooryard where he waited for her, Ruben helped Kathryn to get into the wagon before heading back to the Peters' cabin.

Caroline Peters was indeed a very young woman and this being her first child, Kathryn could tell she was frightened of what would happen once the baby was delivered from her body.

"What can we do?" Edwin asked.

"You can get out," Kathryn replied, as she set the kettle on the hanger in the fireplace to heat the water to boiling. "At a time like this, men are of no help whatsoever. When the child is born, I will let you know. That is when your work will begin, because your wife will need you to care for her as well as the child."

She watched as the men dutifully left the cabin. Once they were gone, she turned her attention to Caroline. "How long have you been having pains?"

"Are you a midwife?"

"Yes I am. My name is Kathryn Clay. My mother was a midwife and she taught me everything she knew."

"Why didn't she come?"

Kathryn could feel the half-truth burning on her tongue. "My mother is dead. I have been lucky to find a home with Ruben and Maude Morton. She is also due to deliver her child soon and I have been helping around the house with her daily chores as well as with the children."

All the time they talked, Kathryn made her preliminary examination of her patient. It was evident Caroline was in the very early stages of labor and the birth was still several hours away. Rather than allow the young woman to lie in the bed, she prompted Caroline to get to her feet and walk around the cabin.

"Are you sure this is good for me?"

"My mother always had the mothers walk around," Kathryn assured her. "It helps the labor to progress if you are active. It is nothing to harm the baby but it will ease your pain a bit."

Caroline nodded and did as she was told. Kathryn smiled to see her instructions were correct as the labor seemed to be progressing quickly. As soon as a pain came, Kathryn insisted Caroline lie back down on the bed until the pain subsided.

"I think it is time for you to lie back down and push. The baby has dropped into position to be born. Soon you will hold your child and this pain will be but a forgotten memory." She thought of Morning Star as she spoke the words she'd heard her mother speak to new mothers so many times in the past.

After pushing hard several times, the baby freed itself from its mother's body and screamed in protest at the air outside the warm womb.

"You have a beautiful daughter," she declared as she held up the screaming infant. Instead of the words of love she expected from the new mother, she heard another scream of pain. Upon checking on Caroline, she saw a second baby making its way into the world.

"You are truly blessed," she said, once the second child and the afterbirth were delivered. "You have a son as a companion to your daughter. Both children are healthy."

"Two?" Caroline questioned weakly.

"Yes, two babies. Among some people twins are considered to be good luck."

"How will I have enough nourishment for two babies?"

"Your body will supply what the children need. I will clean you and the children up, brew you some tea to help you regain your strength, then I will bring your husband to you."

With Caroline and the babies resting peacefully, Kathryn took a moment to reflect on the babies she'd just delivered. Seeing them sleeping in their mother's arms she thought of the brother she'd always considered her twin. Otter Pup was her other half, or so she thought until she learned of her connection to the whites who were coming into the area. She wished her mother never told her of the white parents who gave her life. She wanted her life in the village, her friends and her bother back in her life. As much as she liked Ruben and Maude, they weren't her family. It was the same with Thomas and Leona. They said they were family and they looked like her, but it wasn't the same. She hadn't grown up with them at her side.

A tear of self-pity escaped from her eye and she quickly wiped it away before going out to tell Edwin of the miracle that happened while he waited outside of the cabin.

As soon as she left the cabin, Edwin was immediately on his feet. "Is my wife alright?"

"She is perfect, as are your daughter and son."

"Two? She had two babies?"

"Yes, you have two healthy babies to nurture and love. It is truly a miracle. Twins are special and will give you twice the love."

"You sound like you know what you're talking about."

She thought for a moment before she answered. She did know, but didn't dare say she'd been raised as a twin. "Among our people, there was a family with twins. They were very special and loved by everyone."

Edwin nodded, his smile showing his pleasure at the news of his new babies. "How much do I owe you?"

"Owe? I don't understand what you are saying."

"Have you never been paid for your services as a midwife?"

"It was not so with the people where I was raised."

"Here, a man or woman is paid for the work they do. I have been setting aside money for the midwife. Before she died, the midwife we had in the village told me how much it would be for her to attend the birth of our child. I think it is only proper for me to give you twice that much for two babies."

"But..."

"I will hear no protests from you. Let me fetch the money before I take you back to the Morton farm."

"There is no need for you to take me home. I'm certain Ruben is waiting for me at the local tavern."

"Nonsense. It's getting late. Ruben went home hours ago, to do the night milking. I insist on taking you home."

For the first time, she noted the position of the sun. Being the beginning of autumn, the waning daylight was deceiving. It was evident evening would soon be falling. She wasn't afraid of the dark, nor was she worried about walking back to the farm. It took only a short while for them to come here in the wagon and Ruben hadn't been pushing the horse to more than a leisurely pace.

"You are needed here. I know the way back to the farm and will be able to walk it easily."

"I cannot allow you to walk back alone. Caroline's father does not live far away. If you will stay here, I will go for him. He will know what to do and who to bring to stay with Caroline and the babies while I take you home. I do wish you lived closer to our cabin. Have you ever considered leaving Ruben and Maude? There is a house available as no one has lived in it since the midwife died. There is a great need for a midwife as this is an area of many young couples, many of whom are expecting to have babies soon. You could make a good living and have your own home. Perhaps you should think about it. I'll talk to the leaders and see if they agree with me."

"Thank you, I will."

While Edwin went to get his wife's father, Kathryn returned to the house. Caroline and the babies were all sleeping, giving Kathryn a moment alone to contemplate what it would be like to have a home of her own.

As enticing as the thought of a living in town sounded, Kathryn knew nothing could be decided until Maude's baby was born. They'd taken her in when she had nowhere else to go. She couldn't desert them.

The door of the cabin opened and Edwin returned with Caroline's father.

"We are in your debt, my dear," Caroline's father, John Martin, said. "Edwin told us of your skills and I agree with him, you should live closer to the women who need you. I own the house where our last midwife lived and would be pleased if you would move in. Because of what you have done for my daughter there would be no charge to you. It is completely furnished and with the money you will be making in the future, you would be self-sufficient."

"I don't know. Maude is due to deliver her baby soon. I am indebted to them for taking me in when I had nowhere to go. I couldn't leave until I deliver her child."

"I understand completely. I have decided I will be the one to take you back to Ruben's farm. At that time, I will talk to Ruben and I'm certain we can come to an agreement about this."

Sky Eyes

The shadows of evening were lengthening, making Kathryn wonder how John would make it back to town before nightfall left the track between the farm and town in complete darkness.

As soon as they pulled into the dooryard, Ruben came out of the barn. By this time of day, she knew he'd just completed the evening milking and would be ready for supper.

"Did everything go well?" he asked, once he helped Kathryn down from the wagon.

"It most certainly did," John replied before Kathryn could answer. "Kathryn did an amazing job in helping my daughter to deliver a pair of healthy new grandchildren."

"Twins? Well, I'll be. Since it's getting late, why don't you have supper with us. You can sleep in the loft until morning. I'm certain as late as it is no one is expecting you to get back to town yet tonight."

"I was hoping you'd invite me to stay. There is much I would like to discuss with you and Maude."

Even though she knew what John wanted to talk about, she dreaded the conversation that would follow. Over the time she'd been on the farm, she'd become comfortable. If she was to move into the house in town would she be able to survive on her own?

Thinking about her future, she wrapped her fingers around the small purse Edwin insisted she take in payment for helping Caroline deliver the twins. Having no idea the worth of money, she fingered the coins and slipped them back into her pocket. Once the men were engaged in conversation, she would ask Maude what she actually possessed.

As soon as they entered the cabin, Kathryn sensed something was amiss. Although the stew simmered over the fire, Maude was nowhere in sight.

"Where is your mother?" Ruben asked of his oldest son.

The boy merely pointed to the sleeping area Ruben and Maude shared.

Kathryn could hear Maude moaning softly and went in to check on her. "Are you in labor?" she whispered, so as not to upset the men.

Maude nodded. "I feared you wouldn't get here in time. The pains began while I was making the stew. The birth is still a while away. Can you serve supper?

"Of course I can, but I want to check on you first."

After making her examination, Kathryn agreed with Maude and went into the main living area to serve supper.

"You will have another child before the night is over. I will serve your supper and feed the children before I return to be with Maude. Once you have finished eating, just leave the table as it is. I will clean everything up after the baby is born."

"Are you up to delivering another child after delivering my daughter's twins this afternoon?" John asked.

"I will not be the one doing the work. I will be all right. Maude is my main concern."

She ladled out the stew and helped the children take their places at the table. Once everyone was fed, she returned to where Maude labored to deliver her next child.

~ * ~

"What did you want to talk to me about?" Ruben asked when they stood outside the cabin enjoying their pipes while the children chased fireflies.

"You know the reason we asked Kathryn to come into town was to help Caroline with her delivery. We never thought we would be in the position of looking for a midwife, but as you know we lost the woman who tended to our women's needs. There is a great need for someone like Kathryn in our area. Kathryn told us how she learned midwifery from her mother. Would you be insulted if we were to ask her to move into town and become the midwife for our village?"

"To be truthful, we know very little of her background. She came to us early one morning. It was evident she was traveling alone and perhaps running away from something. All we know is she is an orphan and has no family. Although I don't question her word, I do wonder why someone her age would be on her own. Why is it she doesn't have a husband to care for her? It's apparent something is wrong, but I don't know what."

John ran his hand through his greying hair. "To be honest I don't care about her past. What I do care about is the health of our women. We need a midwife and she is one. I have a house where she can live without thinking about having to pay a landlord. If I'm not mistaken, I'm sure she will be able to care not only for the women in the village but also the minor ailments of the children. She would be an asset to our community and still close enough to be of help to you and Maude if necessary."

~ * ~

Kathryn wasn't surprised at how quickly Maude's labor progressed. What amazed her was the number of children white women produced. The women in the village where she'd been brought up usually had only two to three babies. Limiting the size of their families ensured they would be able to provide enough food for everyone.

Once the men and children left the cabin, she returned to the room where Maude labored in the marriage bed. They had talked about the birthing process ever since Kathryn first arrived, so she knew where to find everything she needed. It was evident Maude had spread a deer skin over the bed earlier so the fluids from the birth wouldn't soil the bedding.

"The pains are coming closer together. I think this baby is anxious to be born."

Kathryn nodded. "I was going to have you get up and walk to hurry along the labor, but I don't think it will be necessary. I can already see the head. It won't be long before the child is born. It is time for you to push."

Maude pushed twice before the child was born. Once the baby gasped for her first breath, she began to cry. There had never been a more welcome sound to Kathryn's ears.

"You have a beautiful daughter," she declared.

"Why wasn't she crying?"

"She only needed to catch her breath," Kathryn explained. Only a moment later, the afterbirth was delivered and Kathryn was satisfied everything was going to be all right.

"I know God brought you to our farm for this reason. Is it possible you will be staying?" Maude stifled a yawn.

"This is something we can speak of at another time. For now, I will get you and the baby cleaned up so the two of you can greet your husband." She could tell Maude was tiring.

As Kathryn cleaned up the baby, she did a quick examination. All of the fingers and toes were in place and the longer the child breathed on her own her skin became a beautifully healthy pink.

Once Kathryn helped Maude into a clean gown and handed her the now sleeping baby, she hurried out to tell Ruben of his new daughter.

~ * ~

Although the work of birthing the baby was done, Kathryn knew there were still things to be done. The deerskin Maude laid on to give birth, as well as the gown she'd worn, needed to be cleaned. It was part of her job to take the soiled garment and the deerskin to the creek where she could cleanse them along with the clothes she'd worn.

Once everything was cleaned to her satisfaction, she dove into the creek to remove any remaining birthing fluids from her body. The chill of the water was in direct contrast to the warmth of evening. She felt blessed to have the full moon shining down on her. It made it easier to find her way back to the cabin.

After hanging the wet clothing on the fence, she started toward the barn. She was exhausted and longed to sleep in her makeshift bedroom in the loft. She was almost to her destination when she remembered Mr. Martin was sleeping in the loft. It certainly wouldn't do for her to be sleeping in the same area as a man. Instead of going into the barn, she decided to lie down on the ground under the large oak tree in the yard, close to the kitchen door. In the past, she'd spent many nights sleeping under the stars. Although she wished she had a blanket, she had no desire to disturb the rest of the people in the house or the barn. Instead, she curled into a tight ball and immediately fell into a deep sleep.

~ * ~

Lukas returned to the Marcus' farm completely devastated. He'd traveled north and then west but no one had seen or even heard of a young woman who could be working as a midwife in any of the settlements he came to. It was as if she'd disappeared into thin air.

"Spend the winter with Emma and me," Markus urged. "With the coming of spring you can resume your search."

"Wouldn't I be intruding on you? I can tell Emma is going to be giving you a child soon. I don't want to be a bother."

"Our brother would never be a bother," Emma said, joining their conversation. "Markus can definitely use help with the farm. We were able to obtain some cattle from a farmer to the south and there is milking to do, to say nothing of putting aside feed for them for the winter. We are thankful for the crops that were planted by Thomas and the others, but they do need to be harvested. Your return at this time is a Godsend."

Lukas tended to agree with his sister-in-law. Just looking around the farmstead he knew what she said was right. Corn grew in the field and was ready to be harvested, while the garden also needed attention it was evident Emma's pregnancy had progressed to the point where she wouldn't be able to tend to it. There was certainly enough work to keep him busy for the winter. There was no sense in leaving during the coldest months of the year. In the spring, he would leave and search to the south. If he didn't find her, he would return and claim the land adjoining Marcus' farm as his own.

Thinking about the quest he would be going on in the spring, he wondered if there would be a midwife to help Emma with the birth.

"Has the settlement gotten someone to be the midwife?" he finally asked.

"Leona's mother is acting as the midwife, only because of her age and past experiences. We have no one trained as a midwife, but I have confidence in Jacqueline's abilities. You'll see, everything will go as planned."

"I understand what you are saying, but I wish Kathryn was here to be with you. I've heard the stories of how she has helped the women in the area where we settled when we originally came to Wisconsin."

Emma took his hand in hers. "I too have heard of her abilities, but she isn't here and we have to make the best of our situation."

CHAPTER TEN

Kathryn stayed on the farm for another two weeks before moving into the small house John Martin offered her in town. For the first time she was truly alone, living in a house all her own.

Little by little she was learning the value of the money people paid her to deliver their babies. With John's help, she was able to put money away while still being able to pay for the things she needed for her daily existence.

Kathryn smiled as she bid yet another young woman goodbye. The woman was in her late teens and expecting her first child. Since her mother had died while in childbirth several years earlier, Patsy Campbell was extremely worried about giving birth. Kathryn couldn't blame her for her fears. Times were different when Patsy's mother died. From what Kathryn heard, she was alone and the birth didn't go well. It would be different with Patsy. Kathryn would see to it when the time came.

She had little time to dwell on Patsy as three children came to her door. One of the boys was crying and there was blood on the knee of one of his pantlegs.

"Timothy, what happened?" she inquired as she ushered the children into her cozy kitchen.

"We were playing and Timothy fell on a rock," Anthony Parsons explained, since Timothy was crying too hard to explain things.

Kathryn helped Timothy to take off his ripped britches and assessed the damage to his knee.

"Anthony, I want you to go to get Timothy's mother. I'll take good care of your friend,"

"I'm going to stay with my brother," Sally Carter declared as she put her hands on her hips and stomped her foot.

Kathryn tried hard not to laugh. She'd seen Irene Carter to do the same thing many times over the past year.

"Of course, you will stay with Timothy. He'll need you to be here with him to help him be strong."

As soon as she talked about strength, Timothy stopped crying and put on a brave front. Carefully, Kathryn cleansed the dirt from the cut on his knee. It was a minor cut and once she had the area cleaned, she was able to apply a soothing ointment she'd made from the healing herbs she'd gathered over the previous summer. Throughout the winter, she'd made several different healing ointments.

"Oh Kathryn, how is my son?"

Kathryn looked up to see Irene Carter enter her house. "He will be fine. I have cleaned the wound and it is minor. It will need to be cleaned on a regular basis. Before you take him home I will make up a jar of ointment for you to use."

"I appreciate what you have done, but where are his pants?"

"They were ripped from where he fell on the rock. I know you are busy with your home and your children, so I will be happy to launder them and mend the tear."

"You are too kind, Kathryn. When my husband returns from hunting, I will make certain he compensates you."

Kathryn nodded. She didn't need to be compensated for helping a child, but she wouldn't turn down a payment either. She knew the Carter's situation and understood money was tight for them. If she was lucky, she would be paid with some of the meat from the hunt.

As she had with the young mother to be, she watched from her doorway until they were safely on their way home.

Lost in her thoughts, she closed the kitchen door and began to prepare the evening meal. As she did, she thought about this place she now called home.

Throughout the winter, she became acquainted with the people of the village. Since they knew nothing of her background, she was accepted. For the first time since leaving the only home she'd ever known, she was making friends among the young women. She often wondered about Thomas and Leona as well as the children. They frequently entered her dreams, but she knew they were better off with her far from their farm. Too many people were quick to judge her by the way she'd been raised, rather than the woman she'd become.

~ * ~

During the winter, Emma gave birth to a healthy baby boy. It was evident to Lukas that his brother's family was now established. It probably wouldn't be long before there were more children. Seeing his nephew only made his quest to find Kathryn all the more important.

Spring finally came and with it Lukas' desire to find Kathryn returned with a vengeance. No matter how much Markus pleaded for him to stay and help with the spring planting, Lukas knew if he stayed to help he would never find Kathryn.

"I have to go and I will be leaving in the morning. I plan to return to the old settlement and follow the lake to the south. It's the only direction I haven't searched. I know I will find her there."

"Why can't you understand she doesn't want to be found?" Marcus argued. "If you remember, the note she left for Thomas and Leona said not to try to find her."

"I don't care. I love her and I'm sure she loves me. If it hadn't been for the accusations Amy made, we would be married by now and working the farm adjacent to yours."

"If that is the case, I wish you God's speed. Should you not be successful, we will be neighbors by the time the snow flies."

The next morning Lukas left and rode toward the old settlement. He thought of how he would react when he saw Amy. He knew she was the reason for Kathryn's disappearance from not only Thomas and Leona's lives but also his own.

It was almost nightfall when he arrived at the village. He was immediately greeted by John Franks, the self-appointed minister for the residents.

"Lukas, it's good to see you. When you left to find Kathryn, I was certain we wouldn't see you again."

"I didn't find her and returned to my brother's farm to spend the winter. I'm coming back to follow the lakeshore to the south in the hopes of finding her. I was hoping I could secure lodging for the night in your village. In that way, I can start fresh in the morning."

"Of course, Lukas. My wife and I would be pleased to have you spend the night at our cabin."

Lukas remembered John's wife was large with child when Kathryn disappeared and he went in search with her. "Won't it be an inconvenience? I mean, your child being so young and all, I'm certain she has her hands full without having an extra mouth to feed at your table for even one night."

Immediately, sadness overcame his friend. "There is no child. The birth was hard and left my wife barren. As for the baby, she lived only long enough to take a breath and then died. I often wondered if things would have been different if Kathryn had been attending my wife when she delivered."

"Is Amy still the midwife for the village?"

"After we lost our daughter, we started hearing stories from several other people in the village about Amy. Just before the first snowfall of last year, a young couple came from the east and decided to settle with us. She said she was a trained midwife. Amy tried to discredit her, but slowly, the women of our village have been calling upon her when they are ready to give birth. Since, she has taken over the majority of Amy's duties. By doing so, fewer and fewer families ask Amy for her help. I have heard rumors of how Amy and her husband are considering moving north of here, where his brother has a farm. I can't say I will be sorry to see them go."

Lukas agreed with John and followed him to the house where he and his wife now lived without the prospect of ever having children to fill their lives with happiness.

John's wife, Marian, welcomed him warmly and gladly set another place at the table. The evening meal consisted of roast chicken, mashed potatoes and gravy, winter squash and freshly baked bread.

"I appreciate you offering me a roof over my head for the night," Lukas said.

"It is so good to see you. Are you still searching for Kathryn?"

Lukas again repeated the story of his search and how he was now going to be going to the south of the settlement and continue his quest to find the woman he loved above all others.

With supper finished, Lukas and John spent the remainder of the evening on the porch enjoying their pipes. For Lukas, it was a rare treat. Even though he enjoyed smoking his pipe in the evenings, during the days and weeks he searched for Kathryn, he wasn't always able to obtain the tobacco to engage in the pleasure.

As he lay in bed, he sent up a silent prayer that his search wouldn't be in vain.

~ * ~

Lukas spent two days searching up and down the shoreline of the lake. At last he came to a farmhouse. These were the first people he'd seen since starting his search to the south.

"We don't get many visitors here," the farmer greeted him. "I see you have come from north of here. Is there any news of the people living there as well as the Indians?"

"I have just left two different communities and there have been no hostilities reported. My brother has a farm to the north and west of here. It's very close to an Indian village, but they have had no problems."

"That's good to hear. I'm told there is a tribe to the west of here, but we've seen no sign of them. My name is Ruben Morgan. I know my wife would be pleased if you'd join us for supper. If you'd like, you can spend the night in the hayloft."

Lukas studied the sky and smiled at Ruben's offer. The clouds that were gathering in the west promised rain before the night was over. He certainly didn't relish spending a night in the open with a storm brewing.

"Can we ask why you are traveling alone?" Ruben asked once they finished eating.

"I'm looking for someone. A young woman I was planning to marry has disappeared. I searched to the north and west just after she left, but was unable to find her. I spent the winter with my brother and his wife. Now I am searching for her to the south."

"A young woman you say. What is her name?"

"It's Kathryn, Kathryn Clay."

The expression on Ruben's face told him the name was one that was familiar to him.

"Maude, did you hear what Lukas just said? He's looking for Kathryn Clay."

"Have you heard of her?"

Maude joined them, wiping her hands on her apron. "Kathryn stayed with us for a while last year. On the day our youngest child was born, she was called into town to help Caroline Peters deliver her twins. When she returned, she helped my wife give birth our daughter."

"Do you know where she is?"

"Of course we do," Ruben said. "She has a house in town. Everyone there loves her. She said she had been orphaned and was looking to begin a new life. We always thought there was more to her story, but we didn't ask."

Lukas told of how Kathryn had been living with her aunt and uncle when an older midwife started spreading ugly rumors about her and that was why she'd run away. What he didn't tell them was her connection with the local Indians. It was evident Kathryn didn't want anyone to know of how she'd been raised.

Sky Eyes

~ * ~

Kathryn finished washing up her breakfast dishes and sat down at the table to enjoy a second cup of tea before she started to work on her sewing. She enjoyed having the money to purchase cloth from the dry goods store and decided to make herself a new dress. As she thought about the pattern she would use, as well as what the finished product would look like, a knock at the door drew her from her mental musings to who might require her help. When she opened the door, she was surprised to see Lukas Palmer standing on her porch.

"Kathryn," he said, tears pooling in his hazel eyes. "I didn't think I'd ever find you."

"What are you doing here, Lukas?"

"I've been searching for you ever since you left. I love you, Kathryn. I want you in my life. There was no way I would have claimed the farm next to Marcus without you by my side."

Kathryn's heart swelled with love. Even though she knew it wasn't proper, she allowed him to take her in his arms and hug her tightly.

"Maybe it would be best if we go inside. I do have a reputation to uphold."

Lukas broke the embrace and allowed her to lead him inside her small house.

"I was about to give up hope. That is until last night when I stopped at a farmhouse. The people there told me they knew you and how you'd recently settled here. I couldn't get here fast enough. I still want you to be my wife. That is, unless you have already taken a husband. I was so excited to learn of your whereabouts, I never thought if you were married."

"I have not married, nor do I want anyone other than you. The problem is I cannot go back with you. Here I have made a life for myself and no one knows of the way I was raised or by whom. I know your dream is to farm close to your brother but I cannot go back there."

"I can farm anywhere. I know your place is here. If I need to, I will find a job in the area. I saw a blacksmith shop when I rode in. My father not only taught me to be a farmer, but also to be a blacksmith. It was something all of my brothers had to learn because our farm was so far from the blacksmith's shop we had to do our own work. I will gladly find a job here if it means you will be my wife and helpmate for the rest of my life."

"You would give up your dream for me?"

"Yes, I would. We are not so far from where my brother and your uncle live that we wouldn't be able to visit from time to time."

Kathryn felt a warm glow fill her entire being. This was what she wanted. She never imagined Lukas would be willing to give up his dream to have her in his life. "Are you certain?"

"I am so certain, I am planning to go to visit the blacksmith and ask him for a job. Once I return to Marcus and Emma's farm for the remainder of my possessions I will come back here and we will be married."

Kathryn felt a knot form in the pit of her stomach. "Will you tell them you've found me?"

"Of course I will. Everyone is worried about you. It was Amy who spoke those terrible things. Everyone is happy she didn't come with them. You are loved there but I can understand the reason you left. Not only were you shamed by what Amy said, I remember how the Indians treated you when they brought you to Thomas to stay. I didn't approve of their actions any more than I did the things Amy said against you. I can understand why you don't want to return and, as I said before, I am more than willing to move here to be with you."

Her heart swelled with love and pride. The people she loved still loved her and even though she couldn't think of returning to them, she knew she wanted Lukas in her life.

"I must tell you, before I began my journey to the south, I stopped in the town close to the lake. It was there I met John Franks and heard that his wife had given birth to a daughter but she died moments after her first breath. He blamed Amy. Luckily, a young couple came to join them and the wife was a trained midwife. There are many who are not happy with Amy. Because of all the talk, as well as her accusations not only about you but also the new midwife, she and her husband are moving north to be closer to his brother. John is certain if you had attended his daughter's birth, she would have lived. Even there, you are remembered and missed."

They talked for several minutes before Lukas left to go to speak with the blacksmith. Alone in her cozy house, she dreamed of the day when Lukas would be sharing it with her. She also thought about what he'd told her. She grieved for the Frank's daughter and prayed Amy would never act as a midwife again.

~ * ~

Lukas left the small house and wondered if he'd done the right thing. He wanted Kathryn in his life but he also wanted to farm close to his brother. Was his love for her enough to override his loyalty to Marcus? The answer was an overwhelming yes, but what would he tell Thomas? How could he make the people understand Kathryn's reluctance to return to them?

The questions continued until he found himself in front of the blacksmith's shop. The man working the bellows wasn't much older than Lukas and for a moment he wondered if this man would be accepting of his quest for work.

"Something I can help you with?" the man asked, his voice carrying a heavy German accent.

"I was wondering if you could use someone to help you?"

Surprisingly, the man broke into a wide grin. "I knew God answered prayers but I didn't know he did it so quickly."

The statement bewildered Lukas. "What do you mean?"

"My papa and I opened this shop. Last week he died suddenly. This is the first day I've had the shop open since we buried him on Saturday. I looked at the amount of work I have to do and I didn't know if I could even think of getting all the orders filled. When can you start?"

Lukas shook his head in disbelief. Everything was happening too quickly. "I-I just located the woman I want for my wife. She doesn't want to leave here and I will be relocating. I have to retrieve my belongings, but

I think I can be here two weeks from today."

"I do need the help, but I can survive for two weeks. My name is Herman Kellogge."

Herman held out his beefy hand.

"Lukas Palmer," he replied as she shook Herman's hand. "I will go and tell Kathryn what has happened and then I will leave to go to my brother's farm to get my things. I will see you two weeks from today and I will be ready to work."

"Kathryn? You mean Kathryn Clay? She is well known around this area. I have always wondered why she had no man in her life. You are a lucky man. A lucky man indeed."

Lukas couldn't believe his good luck. Never in his wildest dreams would he have thought he would find Kathryn and obtain a job on the same day.

After leaving the blacksmith shop, he hurried back to Kathryn's house.

"Can you arrange for our wedding to be held in two weeks' time?"

"What are you saying, Lukas?"

"When I left here I went to the blacksmith shop. I asked if the smithy needed any help and he hired me. I told him I had to go back to my brother's farm to retrieve my belongings. I will be starting work two weeks from today. If I'm working here I will need a place to live and if we are not wed it would be improper for me to live here. I love you Kathryn, will you do me the honor of becoming my wife?"

"Are you talking about Herman Kellogge? When you mentioned finding a job I never thought of him. I should have known he would be looking for help. I attended the funeral for his father several days ago. If you are as good a blacksmith as you say, you will be a Godsend for him. I honestly don't know what to say."

"You don't know what to say about what? Me getting a job or agreeing to marry me?"

For a moment, he was afraid Kathryn would say no, but suddenly her face brightened and she said yes. With her affirmative answer, he pulled her into a tight embrace and kissed her tenderly before leaving for his brother's farm.

~ * ~

Kathryn watched as her now betrothed rode away from her home. With him gone, she wondered if it had been only a dream, but she knew it was real. She would have to have the plans for their wedding in place before his return in two weeks' time.

She was still contemplating everything that needed to be done when there was another knock at her door. Expecting to see one of the children, she was surprised when a man she'd never seen before stood on her doorstep.

"I'm told you're a midwife," he said.

"I am. Can I help you?"

"My wife tells me she is about to give birth. I tried in another town but when I told the woman my wife was an Indian she wouldn't come. Will you come to my farm until she gives birth?"

"Of course I will, but who are you?"

The man seemed to be embarrassed at not introducing himself. "My name is Jed Taylor and my wife's name is Sarah."

"Do you know when she might deliver?"

"I don't know. She said it would be soon and she needed a midwife. Her people are too far away and if you won't come with me, I don't know what I'll do."

Kathryn thought for a moment before answering. "Of course I'll come with you. My name is Kathryn. If you give me a minute, I'll put together my kit and be ready to leave."

She silently prayed she would be back home in two weeks. It was hard telling how long it would be before Sarah delivered, but being an Indian woman, she wouldn't have asked for a midwife if she wasn't close to giving birth to her baby.

By the time she finished packing her kit of herbs and other things she would need for the birth, Jed pulled up the wagon to the front of her home.

Knowing she shouldn't go out of town without letting someone know, she hurried to Caroline Peter's home.

"It's good to see you, Kathryn," Caroline greeted her. "Do you have time for a piece of pie? I just took one out of the oven."

"Another time, Caroline. I came to tell you I am going out of town to deliver a baby and I don't know how long I will be gone."

"Thank you for telling me. I would have been worried if I hadn't seen you in the next few days. Where is it you are going?"

"A man by the name of Jed Taylor came to get me for his wife. She says she is about to deliver."

"I don't think I know them. Of course, there are so many new people moving into the area we don't know everyone now, do we? When you get back, come over and we will have a piece of pie together."

Kathryn left and climbed onto the seat of Jed's wagon. If her upbringing had been different she might have been offended when he made no attempt to help her.

She was unprepared for the length of the trip from town to the Taylor farm. It was early afternoon of the next day when they finally arrived at Jed's cabin. Smoke curled from the chimney, telling Kathryn that Sarah wasn't so far along in her labor she hadn't been able to keep the fire burning and perhaps supper cooking.

Walking into the cabin, she was immediately greeted with the smell of a savory stew simmering over the hearth. The immaculate house told her Sarah took pride in her home.

A moan from beyond the curtained off portion of the cabin led Kathryn to where Sarah labored.

To Kathryn's surprise, Sarah was no older than fifteen or sixteen. He brown eyes denoted her fear at the intensity of her labor.

"I am Kathryn," she said in introduction. "I am the midwife. May I examine you?"

Sarah seemed to understand but answered in her native tongue. To Kathryn's amazement, she understood exactly what the woman was saying, even though the dialect was a bit different than the language she'd grown

Sky Eyes

up speaking, she knew they were of the same people.

"What is your true name?" she asked.

"You speak my language?"

"It is a long story, but yes I do. My true name is Sky Eyes but no one calls me that anymore."

Sarah seemed to relax. "I am Meadowlark, but my husband says I should now be called Sarah. How did he manage to find a midwife who speaks my tongue?"

"No one knows I can speak the language of the people, so it will be a secret between the two of us. How long have you been in labor?"

"Since the midday meal but it just got bad."

Once Kathryn did her examination, she realized the birth would happen within minutes rather than hours or days.

"Things are progressing very well. I will go out and tell your husband he will be a father before it is time for the evening meal."

She noticed something akin to fear in Meadowlark's eyes. "Is this man the husband of your choice?"

"No, but he is the man my father chose for me. I was in love with another…"

A pain cut off Meadowlark's words, causing Kathryn to once again check on her patient's progress. "It is time to push, Meadowlark. This little one is anxious to come into this world."

Meadowlark gave two hard pushes and the head of a squalling baby left its mother's womb, followed quickly by shoulders and the remainder of its body.

"You have a healthy baby boy," she declared.

Once the baby and the afterbirth were delivered, Kathryn wrapped the baby in the blanket that had been laid out for this purpose. She handed the crying baby to its mother and was surprised to see tears falling from Meadowlark's eyes. "Do you think my man will think the boy belongs to him?"

"Are you certain it doesn't?"

Meadowlark nodded her head. "Among our people, it is customary for the woman to be with child before she and her lover are joined. I carried my lover's child when my father gave me to Jed. I made certain we were together as man and wife on the night we were joined. When I told him I carried his child, he didn't question whether it was his or not. I pray to the Great Spirit the child will look like me so he will never know it doesn't belong to him."

"Your secret is safe with me. I will now go out to tell your husband of the birth of his son."

As soon as she cleansed her hands from the birthing, she opened to door to see several braves in the dooryard of the Taylor farm.

"I have come for the woman you stole from me," the man who stood toe to toe with Jed said.

"Your woman is not here," Jed argued. "The only women here are my wife, Sarah, and the midwife, Kathryn."

"You may call her Sarah, but to me she is Meadowlark. We were to be joined until you came and stole her from me."

"We were joined with her father's blessing."

"You took advantage of an old man who was dying. I had planned to ask her father for her hand when I returned from hunting. I killed a deer to give to him along with the three ponies."

Kathryn was surprised to hear Jed conversing in Meadowlark's native language. He was far from an ignorant man if he'd learned the language of the people.

She cleared her throat to make her presence known. "You have a healthy son," she said in English so as not to give away her identity.

Both men turned at the sound of her voice. The other men also looked up as though her voice carried authority. She wondered if any of the men other than Jed spoke English.

"The child is mine," the warrior arguing with Jed said, suddenly reverting to perfect English.

The color drained from Jed's face. "What are you saying?"

"The child Meadowlark carried is mine. My offer of the three ponies was not enough for her father, it is the reason I went hunting. He did not want me to join with his daughter and that is why he gave her to you. It has taken me a while to find where you took her, but I intend to return her and the child back to our village." Again, he was speaking in his native language.

"Her father gave her to me. I paid with trade goods."

"Her father is dead and I am returning your goods to you."

The man turned his attention to Kathryn. "I am known as Wolf's Heart. How soon will Meadowlark and the child be able to travel, Midwife?"

Rather than give herself away, Kathryn answered in English. "She has just given birth. Neither of them will be able to travel for at least two days."

"My woman will be ready to leave before dark."

"I know the midwives in your village would not allow this."

"What do you know of our midwives, white woman?"

Kathryn debated for a moment before she gave away her true identity. Taking a deep breath, she said the words that could either seal her fate or make these men accept her.

Rather than speaking in English, she switched to the one she knew the men were more comfortable hearing. "When I was only days old, my white mother was dying of childbirth fever. My white father had died before I was born. It was then the parents who raised me came and took me with them. My mother was Morning Star, who is a well-respected midwife among the people. My father was Running Deer, who is a hunter for our people. It wasn't until the white men came to our area that they told me of my heritage. When my background became known, I was no longer welcome in the village. I didn't feel welcome with my white uncle and went to where no one knew me. It was there that Jed found me to help his wife with the birth of her son."

She could tell Wolf's Heart was contemplating what she told them. "You will come with us when we leave."

"What about me?" Jed asked. "You can't take my wife."

"We can and we will," Wolf's Heart replied. "If you protest it could cost you your life. I do not want to kill you, but I won't hesitate if it means my woman will not be coming with me. There are other women for you, but Meadowlark is mine."

"What if I call out the military?"

"It is not worth a war. Do you love her?"

Jed hung his head. "I needed a wife and her father agreed to sell her to me. I do not love her."

"Then I am buying her back. She will come with me and so will the midwife. You will retain your life. Other than not having her to warm your bed and cook your meals you will be no worse off than you were when you purchased her from her father."

The conversation was making Kathryn sick to her stomach. "Meadowlark is not property. She is a woman and as such should be cherished. I was raised in a loving home. I do not see where either of you love her."

"That is where you are wrong, Midwife. I have loved Meadowlark since we were children. Since my father was a hunter, her father did not think I was worthy of her. He was one of the elders of our tribe. He is no longer living and she is no longer his to sell to a white man. With me she will be treated with great respect and will never want for anything."

"Then why take me?" Kathryn asked.

"Our people are in need of a midwife. Perhaps one of our men will take you as his wife. If you prefer you could stay here and grace the bed of this man." He pointed toward Jed.

"I am promised to a man who will be coming back to marry me soon. If I'm not there he will come looking for me. I have told people where I am going."

Wolf's Heart laughed at her insolence. "You have no say in where you go, white woman. If I say you go with us that is where you will go. You are far from the whites and by the time someone comes looking for you we will be far from here. For now, I am going in to see my woman and my son."

"You will take her nowhere, Wolf's Heart."

Everyone turned to see Meadowlark standing in the doorway of the cabin.

"She is my friend and she will not be forced away from her people in the same manner as I was forced away from you by my father. You have been good to me, Jed, but the child is not yours. He is Wolf's Heart's son. As Wolf's Heart said, you have your trade goods back. You will take Sky Eyes to her home and tell no one of what has become of me."

Kathryn watched as all of the fight went out of Jed. Even though he didn't love Meadowlark, she could tell he would miss her and had come to care for her.

"Who are you to be telling me what to do?"

"I am your woman and I just gave birth to your son. I will not be able to travel until Sky Eyes says I can, so it is best if you and your men make camp. There is enough stew in my cooking pot for everyone to eat their fill. Until I am ready to travel back to our people, you will treat Sky Eyes with the same respect as you treat me."

Kathryn admired the spunk of the girl who had just given birth. Unfortunately, she saw something else that overrode her admiration. Even from the distance that separated them, she could see the color draining from Meadowlark's face. The exertion of getting out of bed so soon after the birth and confronting the father of her child had been too much for her.

Moving quickly, Kathryn rushed to Meadowlark's side. She no more than put her arm around the younger woman's waist before Meadowlark collapsed.

"What is happening?" Wolf's Heart demanded.

"Your arguing has taken a toll on Meadowlark. She shouldn't have been out of bed this soon. I don't know how much damage has been done. For now, all of you stay outside and allow me to care for my patient."

Turning to Jed she continued. "The stew is ready to be eaten. Go in and bring it out here so all of you men can be fed. Hopefully, you can eat a meal without killing each other. I can see both sides of this argument. I was raised without my family, but I was raised with love. Neither you nor Meadowlark, or as you call her Sarah, admit to loving one another. Is that how you want this child raised? He is not your son and in truth, she is not your woman. You purchased her as if she was a horse or a milk cow. This man loves her and she loves him."

Jed hung his head nodding his agreement. As he came into the house, he took Meadowlark into his arms and carried her to the bed before taking the stew pot from the hanger over the hearth. Once he took it outside, he came back for eating utensils.

Assured she was now alone, Kathryn turned her attention to Meadowlark. She was concerned not only with the color of her complexion but also the amount of blood she was now losing. Under normal circumstances a new mother would rest until at least the next day before getting out of bed, but nothing about this was normal. She was certain there would be no way Meadowlark and the baby could travel to the Indian village for the next several days.

"Am I going to die?" Meadowlark whispered.

"Not if I can help it. You shouldn't have gotten out of bed."

Before the young woman could make further comment, she closed her eyes. Afraid Meadowlark might lose consciousness, Kathryn kept up a constant conversation while she prepared a healing tea. It took several minutes for it to steep, but when at last it was the strength Kathryn desired, she helped Meadowlark into a sitting position so she could sip the tea without spilling any of it.

Several hours passed before the bleeding became normal rather than a hemorrhage. When she was assured Meadowlark slept peacefully, Kathryn took a minute to sit down on one of the two chairs in the cabin.

For the first time, she realized how long it had been since Jed first knocked on the door of her home. They'd left in the early afternoon and traveled throughout the night and until the afternoon of the next day to arrive at the cabin. It was now completely dark and she was certain it was well past midnight.

Sleep came quickly and with it dreams of the future she would share with Lukas once she returned to the little house she loved so much.

Sky Eyes

~ * ~

The crying of the newborn from the curtained off bedroom area brought Kathryn to full awareness. The first light of dawn was showing through the only window of the cabin. Knowing Meadowlark might be too weak to see to the needs of the child, Kathryn got to her feet and lifted the crying infant from the cradle.

Gently she roused the sleeping mother. "Your son needs to be fed," she said as soon as Meadowlark opened her eyes.

"I'm sorry I didn't hear him crying," she replied.

Kathryn wasn't surprised the new mother hadn't heard soft cries of the tiny infant. The healing tea she'd given her was meant to give the young woman the rest and sleep she needed. She watched as the tiny mouth latched onto its mother's breast and sucked greedily. When he stopped, she decided the baby had probably sucked the first breast dry, so she switched him to the other side. It was then that she realized Meadowlark's skin was hot to the touch.

Worried about childbirth fever she allowed the child to nurse while she chose an herb from her kit and mixed up another healing tea, this one to counteract the fever starting to take hold of Meadowlark's body.

When the baby finished and fell asleep, she helped Meadowlark to once again drink the tea. "I feel so hot," Meadowlark said. "Am I dying?"

"No, but you must rest and continue to drink this tea I have made for you."

"Will I be able to leave with Wolf's Heart when the morning comes?"

"I'm afraid not. You will not be able to travel for several days. I will explain things to Wolf's Heart and Jed. It is my prayer they will both understand."

Kathryn wished she was as positive about the outcome of her meeting with the men who slept outside while she tended to the needs of Meadowlark and her son.

With the cabin door open, she could smell the campfire that burned brightly in the dooryard. To her surprise, only the braves who came with Wolf's Heart were there and the wagon was gone.

"Where is Jed?" she questioned.

Wolf's Heart was immediately on his feet. "How is my woman?'

"She is sick. I fear it is childbirth fever. Luckily, I had the correct herbs to heal her."

"The white man left in the night. He took the wagon with him. When I asked where he was going he would not say. I do know he was headed south."

Kathryn's heart sank. Her home lay to the north and the east. How would she ever find her way home?

"When can we leave for my village?"

Kathryn was so engrossed with her own thoughts she missed what Wolf's Heart said.

"Answer me woman. When can I take my woman to my village?"

"She's too sick to travel for several days."

"My men will make a travois and she will be ready to travel as soon as the sun rises completely."

"She must stay here so I can care for her."

"You will come with us and see to the needs of Meadowlark and the child."

By the look on Wolf's Heart's face she knew better than to argue with him. "It will take me a while to prepare the healing tea for the journey. How long will it take for us to get to your village?"

"If we were to ride hard we could be there by nightfall, but going slower will take us two days."

Kathryn was pleased she'd noted the direction the men came from the night before. Even though they were already there when she came out of the cabin, she realized they'd just arrived and their horses had come from the west.

Leaving the men in the dooryard, she returned to the cabin to begin brewing the tea to take with them. While she waited for the water to boil, she found a scrap of paper and the nub of a pencil. She thanked the God of the whites and the Great Spirit that Jed was educated enough to have such things in his home.

In her crude scrawl, she left a note saying she'd been taken by Wolf's Heart and his men to the Indian village; one day's hard riding to the west. Hopefully Caroline would become concerned about her when she didn't return home and send some of the men from the settlement to come to her rescue.

It didn't take long for Kathryn to prepare the tea and get Meadowlark ready for the journey ahead of them. As much as she wanted to protest, she knew it would do no good to argue with any of them men who rode with Wolf's Heart.

"Do you know how to ride woman?" Wolf's Heart asked.

"I have a name. I would appreciate it if you would call me by it."

"You didn't answer my question, Sky Eyes."

She chafed at Wolf's Heart calling her by her childhood name. She'd become accustomed to being called Kathryn, but would tolerate him calling her something other than woman. "Yes, I can ride a horse."

"Good, I brought a horse for Meadowlark, but it is now pulling the travois. You will ride it and carry the child."

Kathryn nodded. She'd seen a beautiful cradleboard in the cabin and would have no problem carrying the child on it. She did worry about riding bareback wearing her dress. When she'd ridden as a child she'd always worn leggings.

CHAPTER ELEVEN

Morning Star sat in front of her lodge, enjoying the last rays of sunlight for the day. As happened so often in the late afternoon, she thought of the daughter she'd raised but gave back to the white family who wanted her.

"You look sad, Mother," Hunting Hawk said as he approached her lodge. "Is there something I can do to take the sadness from your heart?"

"There is no one who can do that. I miss your sister."

Her son's eyes beheld the same sadness as her heart when she talked about Sky Eyes. "I miss her as well, but she is with her people. She was ours for many winters and you know she is no longer welcome in the village. Even the man who was to be her husband has joined with another woman and already has children by her. She is no longer one of us."

"Perhaps she is no longer welcome in our village, but that does not mean I no longer love her. She came to me when I was mourning the loss of my daughter, the twin you never got to know. She needed me and I needed her. It is no different today. I need her."

"What would Father say about this desire of yours?"

"Your father has walked with the ancestors for the past two winters. I have become a burden to you and it is time I found my daughter. Perhaps she will allow me to stay with her."

"If you are certain this is what you want to do, I will take you to her home. I don't want you to leave this village, but at least you will see Sky Eyes one last time."

Sky Eyes

~ * ~

Lukas could see the smoke from the chimneys of the town before he actually entered it. He knew Marcus would be disappointed with his decision to leave the homestead he'd planned to make, to be with Kathryn, but he hoped his brother would understand.

"Lukas, you're finally back," Marcus called as he left his horse in the field he was clearing to be planted once the final grip of winter was gone.

"I am finally back, but not to stay."

"What are you saying? Did you find Kathryn? Is she coming later?"

"I found Kathryn, but she is not coming back. She has found a place where she is comfortable. No one there knows of her background. I have asked her to be my wife.and have found a job at the blacksmith's shop."

"I don't understand. She has family here."

"She also remembers the angry words Amy spoke before you left to come here. She wants no one to know of her childhood spent among the Indians of this area. Knowing how some people feel about the Indians, I do not blame her."

Marcus nodded and headed toward his cabin. "While you were gone, Emma became very sick and died. Even though I mourned her, I have brought Becky Sue into our home to care for our child. She has been able to nurse the boy along with her own child, since her husband was killed in a horse runaway before their daughter was born. Once a proper amount of time has passed, I will make her my wife. It will be good for both of us as well as our children."

Lukas was shocked to learn of his sister-in-law's death. As he thought about it he realized she hadn't ever regained her strength after giving birth to his nephew.

Upon entering Marcus' cabin, he expected to see Emma, but it was Becky Sue who tended to the two babies who were almost the same age. He remembered how she'd given birth to the little girl while still mourning the loss of her husband. As he looked at her, he thought of how Kathryn had been nursed and brought up by someone other than her mother. He couldn't help the parallels he saw in both situations.

The brothers fell into an awkward silence, while Becky Sue served the evening meal. Once grace was said, Marcus turned to his brother. "You said you have a job waiting for you with one of the people living close to Kathryn. What will you be doing?"

"As I told you, I was able to get a job working for the local blacksmith. It was something I always enjoyed doing when we were working with Pa on the farm. I had hoped to open a forge once we were farming together. Kathryn has her own home and that is where we will live."

"She has been able to build a house? How could she do that?"

Lukas pondered his brother's questions. He too wondered about the house where Kathryn lived. "I asked her the same questions. The house belonged to the former midwife. When she became sick and died, the town offered to rent the house to Kathryn. It's small but we could live there comfortably. I hope it is possible for me to be able to buy it once I've become established at the blacksmith shop."

"I'm pleased to think Kathryn has found happiness in her new home," Becky Sue said as the two men enjoyed their meal.

Lukas knew his soon to be sister-in-law was saying only what she thought he wanted to hear. It was evident by the look on her face that she agreed with his brother about not wanting them so far away.

~ * ~

After helping Marcus with the morning chores, Lukas packed his belongings and made his way to let Thomas know he'd found Kathryn and she was doing well.

Upon riding to the area where several houses had been erected, he was surprised to see the woman who had raised Kathryn, along with her son. They were deep in conversation with Thomas but when they saw Lukas, the conversation ceased.

"It's good to see you, my boy," Thomas said, hurrying to his side and pumping his hand. "You remember Morning Star and her son, Hunting

Hawk? They have come to inquire about Kathryn's well-being. Please tell us you've found her."

"I have, Thomas. She is living about a week's ride from here."

"Did she come with you?"

Lukas shook his head sadly. "I came only to tell you about finding her and to get my belongings. I will be going back to make her my wife."

Thomas quickly translated what Lukas told him. As he did, Lukas could see the sadness in Morning Star's eyes. He wished he could tell her Kathryn was going to be closer to her.

The young man said something to Thomas that Lukas didn't understand. Even though he was able to make out most of what was being said, when Hunting Hawk talked so quickly, he couldn't make out every word.

"Hunting Hawk told his mother he would take her to see Kathryn. He wants to accompany you when you go back claim Kathryn as your wife. Would that be acceptable to you?"

"Of course it would. I'd welcome the company on the ride. Tell him if he speaks slowly, we will be able to communicate."

~ * ~

Not being accustomed to riding for long periods of time, every bone in Kathryn's body ached. The only time they stopped was when the baby fussed or Kathryn told them she needed to see to Meadowlark's needs. They'd camped for the night twice and this morning they were again moving toward the west.

She smelled the smoke of the village before she actually saw the lodges dotting the prairie. At each stop along the way she'd checked on Meadowlark and was pleased to see the fever was subsiding. She hadn't realized one of the men had left early and ridden ahead to tell the people of Meadowlark's son, as well as her condition.

They were greeted by several women who were all willing to take over Meadowlark's care, giving Kathryn a needed break. She'd not slept much since Jed first brought her to the cabin to care for his wife.

An older woman came up to Kathryn as soon as she dismounted. "I am Caring Woman, the sister of Meadowlark's mother. I am told you are called Sky Eyes and you speak our language. Her father had no right to sell her to the white man. White Owl came to tell us of how you saved both her and her child."

"I only helped her with the birth. I was lucky to have had the proper herbs in my kit to counteract the childbirth fever. Had she not tried to stop the argument between Wolf's Heart and the man called Jed and rested as she should have after the birth, she wouldn't have become so sick. Surely your midwives will be able to take over her care?"

"Were you not told our midwife has died and the young woman she was training would not have known what to do for Meadowlark? Since we have been told you are a trained midwife, we need you to take her place and at the same time train the two young women who want to serve the women of our village."

"You don't understand. I must go home. My man is coming to marry me. I need to be there when he arrives."

"You are also needed here. Once you train our young women, our men will take you back to your white settlement."

Kathryn never felt such despair. She'd lived in the white world so long she wondered if she could return to the life she'd lived all through her childhood.

~ * ~

To Lukas' surprise the closer they got to where Kathryn lived, the closer he became to both Morning Star and Hunting Hawk. The young man was determined to grant his mother the one wish she had above all others, even if it meant traveling far from his home.

As soon as they rode into the heart of the town, Lukas knew something was wrong. Many of the villagers were gathered outside of their homes and appeared to be in deep conversation. As soon as they were spotted, Lukas saw Herman Kellogg approach them.

"Have you come back for Kathryn?" he asked.

"You know I have. I don't see her, where is she? I have brought some of her friends from the Indian village close to the settlement where we were planning to live before she came here."

"She told me she was going to help with the birth of Jed Taylor's wife," Caroline said, also coming to his side. "When she didn't return, one of the men who knew Jed rode out to his place. When he got there, he found the farm deserted. He did find this note from Kathryn." She thrust the note into his hand.

"What does it say?" Hunting Hawk questioned.

"Taylor's wife was from an Indian village to the west of where the farm was located, and the men from that village took her as well as Kathryn with them."

He could feel the anger rising within the young man as well as the older woman.

"We will go and bring her back where she belongs," Hunting Hawk declared. "I know of this village where she has been taken. I know we have been riding for two days. I am certain she is safe. We will camp outside of town and start fresh in the morning. We have a long ride ahead of us."

The villagers were looking to Lukas for answers. "Hunting Hawk came here in search of Kathryn. Her disappearance has upset him. He wants to camp outside of town and leave first thing in the morning."

"I will be going with you," Herman said.

A glance at Hunting Hawk told Lukas to decline the offer of the man who would someday be his employer.

"Tell the man the more whites who go with us the harder it will be to bring Sky Eyes back to this village."

Hunting Hawk's statement told Lukas the young man understood more English than he'd given him credit for earlier.

"Hunting Hawk says it is best if the three of us go alone."

"Even the woman?"

"Yes. She is the one who wanted to find Kathryn. It would not be right to leave her behind. I also think the people here would be more comfortable if she were with us and not thought of as a threat. We will leave in the morning and with luck we will return with Kathryn."

Lukas knew the men who wanted answers were both upset and relieved. If it weren't Kathryn who was missing, he would be reluctant to go on this rescue mission.

Rather than continue to stay in Kathryn's house, Lukas, Hunting Hawk and Morning Star headed west. There were still several hours of daylight and they could easily put some distance between themselves and civilization before making camp for the night.

"Just how much English do you know?" Lukas asked Hunting Hawk as Morning Star prepared the squirrels they'd killed once they camped.

"Not enough to be comfortable speaking it, but I did sense the people in the village we just left think highly of my sister and not so highly of my mother or myself. I've learned much of your language from the people at the trading post. The man who runs it is honest and he has taken the time to learn our language. It is only right we should learn his. Perhaps when we find Sky Eyes, the two of you can teach both my mother and myself enough so we can be understood by the whites."

"I understand your discomfort. I have to admit, I was afraid to travel with the two of you, but I've come to know and respect you both. You love her as much as I do. I'm sorry she was taken from you in the way she was. It is sad that children know no difference between Indian and white and it is only when they become adults that the hatred and prejudices take hold. As for teaching you English, it would be my pleasure."

Once they finished eating their evening meal, Lukas began the first of many lessons he would give to Hunting Hawk and Morning Star.

CHAPTER TWELVE

Kathryn was amazed at how quickly she adapted to life in Wolf's Heart's village. She learned more of the distrust between Meadowlark's father and the man she loved.

This village was so different from the one where she grew up. In her village, there would never have been a divide between the elders and the hunters. Everyone was equal. As for the fact there was no midwife, that too would never have happened. Young women began training at an early age and were capable of carrying out any duties necessary by the time they themselves became adults.

The two young women who were training with the midwife before her death, were well meaning, but they didn't have the abilities necessary to do the job correctly. It was up to Kathryn to teach them everything she knew and ask them to assist her with the duties of a midwife on two occasions since her arrival in the village.

She wished it was springtime rather than fall. In the springtime, she would be able to gather the roots and herbs she needed for the healing teas. It was true she had several with her but they would never be enough to last throughout the entire winter. Once her supply was gone, would these people allow her to live? She highly doubted it.

Kathryn thought about how long she'd been gone from the town. Jed arrived at her home only hours after Lukas left to go north. She calculated the amount of time Lukas had been gone and realized he would already have arrived to find her home empty. Would he ever be able to find her again? It was possible too much time had passed for him to even begin to follow her trail.

It was a beautiful fall day and time for Kathryn to take her students into the forest in search of fall herbs. It was true they weren't the same ones she enjoyed finding in the spring, but they would have to do.

"Sky Eyes, wait up."

Kathryn turned at the sound of Meadowlark's voice. During the time she had been in the village, the young woman had made a miraculous recovery. It was good to see her looking healthy and being able to care for her son.

"What can I do for you, Meadowlark?" Kathryn asked when at last the young woman caught up with them.

"I was wondering if I am too old to also train with you to be a midwife. I would have never been able to do the things you did for me. I feel this is something I want to do."

"What does Wolf's Heart say of this? Since the two of you were joined as soon as you arrived in the village, you must abide by his wishes."

"We have talked about it and both agree that perhaps it would be best if more of the women in the village knew of the skills you have."

"It is best if we think about this. You are still recovering from the birth of your son and have yet to give him a name. It is not that I do not want to teach you, I just feel you need more time to heal and to be a wife."

"We have talked about that as well. Since Wolf's Heart is responsible for his mother now that his father walks with the ancestors, she has agreed to take over the duties of cooking for our family, while I train with you. As for the baby, he will be named at the time of the next new moon and I will have him with me. We are doing this for our people."

Kathryn could tell Meadowlark was sincere. "Then why don't you join us as we go into the forest looking for fall roots and herbs? We will not venture far and the fresh air will be good for both you and the baby."

Although Kathryn saw the child on a daily basis, she always enjoyed having the opportunity to check him over. Since the night of his birth, he'd filled out and his little cheeks were definitely full. It was a good sign that the fever his mother experienced right after giving birth had not affected the amount of milk she was able to produce for the boy.

To her delight, he reached out and grasped her finger, warming her heart. If she hadn't been brought to this village, she knew she and Lukas would have been married by now. If they were, it was entirely possible she would already be expecting their first child.

How foolish I am being, she thought. *Many times, it takes several months for a woman to become heavy which child after taking a man to her bed. I know many women who never conceive. What if I am one of them? Would Lukas still want me if I were barren?*

She put such thoughts out of her head. This was her life now and she doubted Lukas would ever be able to find her. The prairie was a vast place and he would have no idea in which direction to go in order to find her. Even if he did, she doubted Wolf's Heart would allow her to leave. For all the freedom she enjoyed, he'd made it perfectly clear that she was his prisoner and would do his bidding for as long as he deemed it necessary.

Already he'd made suggestions of many of the young men who were interested in taking her as their wife. They didn't care she was white. They only wanted one thing from her and that was the one thing she was unwilling to give to someone she didn't love.

~ * ~

The journey Hunting Hawk thought would only take four days now stretched into a journey of over two weeks. Lukas had no delusions about the reason for the delay. Morning Star was no longer a young woman and she didn't have the stamina of her much younger son. They made frequent stops to accommodate her needs. It gave her a chance to get off the horse and walk around.

Even though Lukas wanted the journey to come to an end so he could be reunited with Kathryn and finally make her his wife, he tolerated the stops. He understood the needs of Morning Star. The elderly needed to move at a slower pace, even if it annoyed the younger men traveling with her.

They were just finishing their morning meal and preparing to continue their journey when four riders approached their camp.

"We must be close to the village and have been seen by their scouts. If I am not mistaken, the man coming toward us is Wolf's Heart, the name Sky Eyes wrote in her note," Hunting Hawk observed.

"Do you know him?"

"I do. Many seasons ago our two villages were closer together and my father and I often joined their hunters. We are close to the same age, but he is a much more accomplished hunter than I am. If Sky Eyes is indeed in his village she is not there willingly. It is possible he sees her as his captive. We will have to choose the words we speak to him carefully."

The riders came closer and Lukas watched as the leader of the group dismounted and approached them.

"Hunting Hawk, why have you come close to my village with an old woman and a white man?"

"We have come to bring my sister back to where she is needed. The old woman you speak of is my mother and the white man is the man my sister is to marry."

"I have no woman from your people within my village. Besides what woman of the people would willingly join with a white man?"

"As you well know, my sister is white. She was rescued by my mother when her mother died of childbirth fever. We know her as Sky Eyes, but this man calls her Kathryn."

"There is a white woman in our village. I claimed her when I went to the white man's cabin to bring my woman home. She was stolen from me and I took the white woman in retaliation. She is my property, my slave."

"She is no man's slave," Morning Star declared, angry sparks flying from her eyes. "She is the daughter of my heart if not of my body. She was raised to be a free and independent woman."

"You are far too outspoken for my liking, old woman. Perhaps the men in your village don't teach their women to be respectful. The women in my village know their place and do not talk back to their men."

"This could be because your women are afraid to speak their minds," Lukas said, surprising Wolf's Heart with his mastery of their language. "You said you went to the farm of Jed Taylor to bring back your woman. I am sure your anger was fueled by the fact she was taken from you. Now you must know how I feel. I returned to my woman's home to take her as my wife. When I arrived her friends told me she had been taken captive and brought to your village. I want to see her now so I can see for myself she hasn't been harmed while with you."

"I am not a hard man. I do not harm my captives. There is a need for her among our people. Until she has trained some of our young women to take her place she will remain with us."

"I said it before, I have come a long way and demand to see my woman. I do not want to fight you. If anything, I would like to call you friend in the same way as Hunting Hawk does. There is no reason for us to be enemies."

The look on Wolf's Heart's face seemed to soften. "You are right, white man. I do know how you are feeling. I will allow you to see her but not to take her away from my village."

Lukas made no reply. He knew he needed to choose his battles and this was one he wasn't prepared to fight at this time.

~ * ~

With their baskets filled with herbs and roots, Sky Eyes and the three other women made their way out of the forest. It had been a long day, but a productive one. She'd made certain each of the women knew the use of the roots and herbs they'd harvested. It wouldn't be long before Sky Eyes was confident the women were capable to doing the necessary work of being midwives without her guidance. Once their knowledge was acknowledged, she prayed Wolf's Heart would allow her to return to her home.

As soon as they entered the village, she could see visitors had arrived. Among the darker skinned people gathered around the new arrivals, she saw a white man. To her delight, she recognized Lukas, but knew better than to run to the comfort of his loving arms. Her position as a captive and perhaps even a slave was evident, even if Wolf's Heart said nothing about it. She doubted if she would ever be able to leave the village. Even though she prayed for Wolf's Heart to release her, she knew it was little more than empty hope.

It took only a moment for her to recognize the people with Lukas. The last people she ever though she would see were Morning Star and Hunting Hawk. If they were here, where was the man she'd called father all her life?

"There she is, white man," she heard Wolf's Heart say. "Now that you have seen her you are free to leave."

"I will not leave without her."

"She is my slave and I say she cannot leave my village."

Wolf's Heart's use of the word slave hit her like a slap in the face. Even though she knew that was how he thought of her, hearing the word spoken aloud hurt more than any punishment she might have received if she tried to leave.

"Kathryn is no man's slave," Lukas protested. "She is the woman I love and I plan to take her back to her home."

"She is needed here. Our village has no midwife."

"Then I will be your midwife," Morning Star declared.

"Mother," Hunting Hawk exclaimed. "How could you consider such a thing?"

"The younger midwives in our village have said they no longer need my help or my guidance. I have taught them everything I know. With no mate to bring me meat from the hunt, it is possible I will die when the winter comes upon us."

"You know I will provide for you. This is foolishness," Hunting Hawk protested.

Kathryn agreed with Hunting Hawk. These were not Morning Star's people. How would they treat her? Would she be an honored elder or a slave to do Wolf's Heart's bidding? Even if her mother stayed in the village would Wolf's Heart allow her to leave with Lukas? All of her questions held no answers.

Rather than dwelling on what could be, she focused on Lukas. Had it only been a matter of weeks ago, when he found her and professed his love? It felt like a lifetime passed. Even though she didn't think anyone from the white people who lived in the north would ever find her, she realized he'd searched ever since her disappearance.

Now it seemed as though they would never be together again. Wolf's Heart took her to be his slave. He'd treated her with kindness, but she knew if she tried to leave all of that could change.

"What your mother says has merit," Wolf's Heart said, breaking into Kathryn's silent thoughts. "I have seen older women in my village take their own lives rather than live without their mate. It is evident your mother wants more out of life than to take the gift given by the Great Spirit. She wants to be useful, even if the midwives of your village no longer appreciate her assistance. I will take her suggestion under consideration. For now, you, Hunting Hawk, and your mother will be guests in my village."

"What of the white man who traveled here with us to find his woman?"

Kathryn watched as Wolf's Heart's expression changed from welcoming host to enemy.

"He is not welcome here. The whites are our enemy. Did not a white man steal my woman and take her far away from my village? How do I know he will not try to steal my slave and take her in the same way?"

"She is no one's slave. Kathryn is my woman. I returned to where she lived to make her my wife. I have searched long and hard for her. You have done to me what another did to you. I plead to you man to man. I may be white, but I understand your feelings when your woman disappeared from your village."

Kathryn held her breath as she watched the expression on Wolf's Heart's face. It was true the whites wronged him, but hadn't he done the same? Meadowlark came with him willingly, but Kathryn hadn't wanted to accompany them. It wasn't that she didn't like the women of this village and those who agreed to train with her had become close friends. Being white, she didn't belong here anymore than she had belonged in the village where she'd been raised once everyone knew what made her different from them.

As much as she wanted to speak to her mother, brother and Lukas, she held her tongue. Even though Wolf's Heart hadn't punished her since her arrival, she knew her situation could change at any moment.

~ * ~

Lukas could feel his heart break. Even being with Hunting Hawk and Morning Star, he was outnumbered by the men of Wolf's Heart's village. As much as he wanted to grab Kathryn and make his escape, he knew to do so would mean he would forfeit his life. It was even possible Kathryn would be killed or severely injured. The thought of anyone doing harm to her tore at his heart and kept him from stealing her away.

"I will not enter your village, but I will not be far away. If I find you have harmed her, I promise you I will extract revenge, even if it means I will certainly lose my life. This is the woman I love and have searched forever since she left our people. Be assured, Wolf's Heart, I will be watching you."

Lukas mounted his horse and rode to the east and away from the village. Instead of going too far away he stopped at the campsite where they'd spent the night before riding toward Wolf's Heart's village. It was close enough that he could easily go to the fringes of it and make certain no harm came to Kathryn.

Even during the confrontation with Wolf's Heart, he'd been scouting the area. Although the village itself sat in a clearing, there were enough forested areas around it to give him a secure place.

He gathered wood and built up the fire in the same area where they'd made their campfire the night before. The fire fueled the anger that pumped through his mind. Wolf's Heart knew he was in the wrong by not allowing Kathryn to come back with him. He'd searched for her for too long to lose her now because of some Indian who thought he could take Kathryn prisoner and turn her into a slave. It wasn't right, and he wasn't going to stand for it.

CHAPTER THIRTEEN

Morning Star held back the tears that threatened to spill from her eyes at the sight of her beautiful daughter. Rather than wearing a dress, leggings, and moccasins like the other women who were with her, she wore a white woman's dress and shoes. Morning Star was certain this is the dress she'd been wearing when she was taken to Wolf's Heart's village. There was no reason the inadequate clothing she wore had not been replaced with something more suitable. The warm southern breezes had already been replaced by colder ones coming from the north. Even though the days were warmed by the sun, the nights were cold and soon there would be ice on the edges of the stream and frost on the ground.

"Do you see how your sister is dressed?" she asked Hunting Hawk. "What manner of man does not give even a slave adequate clothing?"

"You know Wolf's Heart is not of our village. Perhaps it is possible the customs these people follow are different from ours. If you plan to stay here and take Sky Eye's place, it is best if you do not voice your opinions too loudly."

"Then perhaps you should be the one to point this out to Wolf's Heart. We have felt the bite of the north wind ever since we left the white settlement. Soon the strong winds of winter will bring snow. With a dress, like the one she is wearing, she will certainly suffer from the cold."

"When the time is right, I will speak to Wolf's Heart. For now, let us not make ripples in the stream. It is enough that we are able to see her. Let that be enough until the time is right."

Sky Eyes

Morning Star didn't agree with her son, but held her tongue. Instead she hurried to her daughter's side.

"Has this man injured you?" she asked, her voice hardly louder than a soft whisper.

"No, Mother. He has not hit me and gives me adequate food."

"Why hasn't he given you adequate clothing?"

"Even though he has not spoken the words until today, I have always known he considers me his slave. I am never allowed to leave the village alone. Even when I go into the woods to gather healing herbs I know there are men who follow me. I am always with the other young women who are training to be midwives but I feel as though I am being watched. Wolf's Heart will not allow me to leave. I cannot allow you to sacrifice your life for something unattainable. If you were to stay we would each become salves and you need to be with Hunting Hawk."

"Your brother does not need me and you do. I will not rest until you are reunited with the man who loves you."

During the trip between the white settlement close to her home and Wolf's Heart's village, she had come to like and respect Lukas. He was a good man and she knew he loved Sky Eyes above all others. Why else would a man search so long and hard for her daughter? The man had a good heart. She would be proud to call him son when and if he and her daughter were together as husband and wife.

"What do you know of Lukas?" Kathryn questioned, her voice hardly more than a whisper.

"I know he is a good man. When we went to where the whites are living close to our village, we were told she was no longer among them. It was Lukas who told us of the life you were living among your friends and how much he loves you. During the time we traveled to find you, he learned more and more of our language. I was pleased your brother knows enough of the white man's tongue that we could communicate. Did you not see the love he had for you turn to anger when Wolf's Heart said he would not allow you to leave his village? He will have you as his wife or he will lose his life in trying to free you from Wolf's Heart's hold."

"I love him as well. I was a fool to leave my white aunt and uncle, even though he'd proclaimed his love for me."

"Then why did you leave? I have been told of the love Thomas and his family has for you. What happened to turn you from them?"

"In the place where I stayed with Thomas and his family, there was another midwife. Although I had the skills, I did not use them until Thomas' wife was giving birth. The babe was turned sideways and the woman attending to Leona would have allowed both the mother and child to die. I turned the baby and removed the cord from around his neck. I also gave Leona healing herbs brewed into a tea to slow the bleeding and restore her strength. Not only did the white midwife take the child to a woman who was nursing, she spread terrible stories about me. On the night before we were to leave for the new settlement, I overheard her once again spreading words of how I would murder them all in their sleep. It was more than I could stand. As soon as the entire household slept, I packed my belongings and left."

"Did you not consider the man who loved you?"

"I considered nothing other than the hurtful words spoken against me. Had it not been for the farmer and his wife who offered me shelter, I would not have found my place in the town where Lukas found me. The Great Spirit and the God of the whites have both smiled upon me. That is until I went to help with a birth and became Wolf's Heart's slave."

Sky Eyes' words tore at Morning Star's heart. She knew how she felt when the younger women of the village told her she was too old to be of any use as a midwife. Their words also tore at her heart, making her feel useless to her own people. How much more damaging would the words of the white midwife have been to her daughter?

~ * ~

Hunting Hawk left his mother and the woman he'd called sister for most of his life and made his way to the lodge of Wolf's Heart. As had his mother, he'd noticed the condition of the dress Sky Eyes wore. It was shameful for someone of the people to treat anyone in such a way, even a slave. She should be allowed adequate clothing, to say nothing of shelter. Thinking about the way she was dressed made him wonder where she spent the nighttime hours. It was entirely possible she slept without shelter. With the coming winter, he worried about her as well as his mother if she were to stay in this village to take Sky Eyes' place.

"I wondered how long it would take for you to come to my lodge," Wolf's Heart said, breaking into Hunting Hawk's private thoughts. "If you have come to ask me to release my slave, you are wasting my time."

"You know that is one of the reasons I have sought you out. You must know Sky Eyes and I were raised as brother and sister even though her skin is white rather than red. The bonds we made as children were ripped from us when my mother admitted her daughter was white and she'd brought her to our village in order to save her life. Seeing her today strengthened the bond we once had. I am concerned with her clothing. You must be able to see it is inadequate for the coming cold weather."

"My slave is white, you have confirmed it. She lives with the whites and wears their clothing. I can see no reason to give her anything other than what she was wearing when she came to us."

"You know that is not the way our people treat their captives or even their slaves. If you are so unconcerned about the clothing she wears, I must ask, where does she spend the nighttime hours? Is she allowed to sleep in a lodge or do you make her sleep with the camp dogs?"

"What you think does not bother me. I will tell you she sleeps comfortably in the lodge of the midwives. That is not to say she is not guarded day and night. Who knows what she would do if she were free to roam the village? I have heard of the destruction brought about by the whites upon the eastern tribes. It is possible she would murder us all in our sleep if she were not guarded."

"Now you sound like the whites who drove her from their midst. I did not allow my mother to know why she ran from those who claimed her but Lukas did tell me it was because they were worried about her killing them in their sleep because she was raised in our village. It shames me to consider you as one of the people. It is no wonder the whites call us savages. If it is the last thing I do I will free my sister from your village."

"If you do, you will lose your life. You say I shame you, but I say the same thing about you. Any man of the people who claims a white woman as his sister has gone soft against the enemy."

Hunting Hawk could think of no civil words to respond to Wolf's Heart. The man's heart had been hardened against the whites, unlike those of the men in his village. Since the coming of the whites close to their village, they'd learned these men wanted only to live in peace close to the area where Sky Eyes' true parents were buried.

Defeated, he made his way back to where he'd left his mother in conversation with his sister. To his surprise, they were not where he'd left them.

"Where is the woman Wolf's Heart is holding as a slave?" he asked of one of the men.

"I see no reason why I should answer your question, but she has gone to the lodge of the midwives with the woman who came with you. One of the women came to them saying Sweet Dove is having trouble birthing her baby."

Knowing he would not be welcomed at the lodge of the midwives, he went back to where he'd picketed his horse. It was best if he sought out Lukas and told him of the conversation he'd shared with Wolf's Heart.

~ * ~

Lukas had been able to shoot two rabbits and had them roasting on the spit over the fire he'd built up earlier when Hunting Hawk rode into camp.

"I see you were telling the truth when you said you would not be far from Wolf's Heart's village," Hunting Hawk greeted him.

"I refuse to lose Kathryn to the devil who holds her as his prisoner."

"I understand your feelings, but it is time for you to return to the settlement where there are people who care for her. It is evident Wolf's Heart is a hard man and he will not barter with you for her release. I will remain here until the cold winds make it impossible. I am certain no harm will come to Sky Eyes during the winter. In the spring, I will return with many braves from my village and if she has not been released by then, we will take her by force."

Lukas took a moment for Hunting Hawk's words to sink in. He'd been a peaceful man all of his life and the thought of violence in order to bring Kathryn back to him sickened him.

"The hour is late," Lukas said. "It is best if we partake of the evening meal. As much as I hesitate in leaving Kathryn in that village, I will do as you say and leave for the settlement in the morning. The people there deserve to know what has happened to her in the past month. You are right when you say Wolf's Heart will not negotiate anything with me. His distrust of the whites was more than evident when we were in his village. I know you are a good man and will do everything in your power to gain Kathryn's freedom."

Lukas could see the relief in Hunting Hawk's eyes. It was evident his presence was not going to make things easier for Hunting Hawk as he met with Wolf's Heart to gain freedom for Kathryn.

~ * ~

Kathryn watched as Hunting Hawk engaged in conversation with Wolf's Heart. She prayed their negotiations would go well. Hopefully, he would return and tell her she was free to go back to Lukas.

"Sky Eyes, you must come to the midwives' lodge. Sweet Dove is ready to give birth. She has been with us for a long time, but the babe is reluctant to be born. We need your help."

Immediately, Kathryn forgot everything but the needs of the young woman who was having her first child. Usually first labors were long but this one was completely unexpected. The child was so anxious to be born it was over a month early. In cases like these, the babe came quickly, making her believe there was something terribly wrong.

The scent of herbs assaulted her senses as soon as she and her mother entered the lodge. On a bed of furs covered with the skin of a deer, she saw Sweet Dove writhing in pain with sweat drenching her body.

"How long has Sweet Dove been here?" she asked one of the women attending the laboring woman.

"She came to this lodge early this morning, before you and the others left to go into the forest to gather roots and berries."

"Why wasn't I advised of this before now?"

The women looked from one to the other. "At first you were in the forest. When you returned, the white man, the young brave and this woman came to the village." The woman pointed toward Morning Star.

"She has a name. It is Morning Star and she is the woman who raised me when my white parents died. It is because of her that I have the skills of a midwife. Allow both of us to examine Sweet Dove."

Apprehension filled Kathryn as she approached the birthing bed. Sweat beaded on the young woman's forehead. While Morning Star checked the progression of the birth, Kathryn wondered if the child would survive or if it had died within its mother's body. If that was the case, Sweet Dove's body would be rejecting the dead child.

""Have you brewed a tea that will hasten this birth?" Morning Star inquired.

The women looked at each other with puzzled expressions. Kathryn couldn't believe what she was seeing. Only days earlier she'd told them of the proper herbs to bring a woman's labor to conclusion. Could they have forgotten everything she told them so quickly?

"I will brew the tea, Mother," she replied.

Once the tea steeped to Kathryn's satisfaction, she took the cup to her mother so Sweet Dove could sip it. Even though the girl was weak from the prolonged labor, she was able to drink the tea and to relax in Kathryn's arms.

Less than an hour passed before the screaming infant made his presence known. As soon as Morning Star assessed the health of the child she handed him to the women who were in attendance. At least they would be able to handle cleaning his tiny body.

"My baby," Sweet Dove whispered. "Is he all right?"

"He is perfect, even though he is very small. He will grow up to be a strong brave who will make you proud."

The women returned the baby to Kathryn's arms. The tiny boy child voiced his protest of not being fed, prompting her to place him in his mother's arms so he could find her breast in order to nurse.

"Your son is hungry, Sweet Dove. It is a good sign. Once he is nourished he will sleep and so will you. I will send one of the women to Buffalo Hunter with the good news."

As soon as the baby contently sucked at his mother's breast, Morning Star pulled Kathryn to one side. "Why did you send one of the other women to tell the father of the birth of his son? They had nothing to do with it. It was because you and I knew what to do that he was finally brought forth from her body. If it had been left to them, they would have allowed her, as well as her son, to die."

"Even though Wolf's Heart hadn't spoken the words about my position with these people, I knew I was a slave and as such, I knew my place. I have no use except to help women birth their babies. It is not my place to speak with the men of this village."

"That is nonsense and you know it. In our village, even our slaves are allowed to speak with anyone in the village. You also know after a certain amount of time they regain their freedom. At that time, they can either be returned to their people or stay with ours. I have never known of a slave who hasn't made the decision to remain in our village. I cannot see anything like this happening here. I am afraid you are trapped."

"I feel the same way, but I also don't want you to be trapped with me. Your generous offer is wonderful, but I do not think it is wise for you to become a slave to these people, since it will not gain my freedom."

She knew her mother was torn but she'd made the decision and Kathryn knew Wolf's Heart would, more than likely, hold her to it.

CHAPTER FOURTEEN

Early the next morning, Lukas prepared to break camp. The thought of returning without Kathryn weighed heavily on his heart. He trusted Hunting Hawk but at the same time wondered how he would explain Kathryn's absence to her friends and neighbors. He also wondered if he would still have a job with Mr. Kellogge if Kathryn did not return with him.

"I fear I must leave both my mother and my sister in Wolf's Heart's village for the winter," Hunting Hawk said. "I will stay and try to get Wolf's Heart to release both of them, but once the snow begins to fall, I will have to return to my own village."

"I trust you will do what is best for Kathryn. I pray you will stop to let me know what is going on before you return to your home." Lukas clasped Hunting Hawk's hand. He trusted this young man and knew he was doing what he felt was best.

~ * ~

It took two days of hard riding, but at last Lukas arrived at the home Kathryn had lived before she was summoned out into the country to attend to a birth. How he wished she had told the man no, but he also knew it was not in her nature to deny anyone who needed her help.

Before going to her house, he made his way to the blacksmith shop to see if Herman had replaced him or if he still had a job.

"Lukas, it is good to see you," Herman said as he wiped his soot covered hands on his leather apron before shaking Lukas' hand. "I was afraid you wouldn't be coming back to me."

"Can I assume you have not given the job to anyone else?"

Herman broke into a wide grin. "I can't say the thought hadn't crossed my mind, but there is no one in the village as qualified as you are. Besides, even though some people have helped me out, they are not willing to work for me all the time. Where are my manners, is Kathryn with you?"

Lukas felt a lump forming in his throat. He swallowed it down in order to proceed. "I'm afraid not. Wolf's Heart is holding her as a slave in his village. I think it is time you know the whole story about Kathryn."

For the next half hour, he told Herman the story of Kathryn's life. He prayed the fact she'd been raised by Morning Star and her husband would not tarnish her in the eyes of these people.

"That's quite the story. I can understand why you came here with the Indian woman and the young man. Is she Kathryn's mother?"

Lukas nodded. "She is the woman who raised Kathryn and taught her the skills of being a midwife. Now I am afraid they are both prisoners in Wolf's Heart's village. The young man is Hunting Hawk and was raised as Kathryn's brother. He is trying to negotiate her release with Wolf's Heart. Whatever happens, he has promised to come to me before the snow flies to let me know what is happening, both good and bad, before he returns to his village."

"I am sorry to hear of this, my friend. Work can wait. For now, I think we should go to the village council and let them know what is happening. Be assured, no one here will hold any of this against Kathryn, or you for that matter. What has happened has happened. We will all have to learn to deal with it."

Lukas thought the day would never end. First, he'd told his story to Herman, then to the council, and finally to a meeting of all the people in the settlement. If he thought these people would react in the same manner as Amy Totten had so many months ago, he was wrong. Here, Kathryn was loved and respected. There was no doubt once her release was negotiated by Hunting Hawk, either by peaceful or forceful measures, she would be welcomed back into the community with open arms.

~ * ~

It was late November. Lukas had been working for Herman for over a month and still there had been no news of Kathryn, either from Hunting Hawk or from anyone else.

The first flakes of snow started to fall as Lukas made his way back to the house where he'd planned to live with Kathryn as husband and wife. As usual he was met by one of the women. Since his arrival, the women told him they would bring him his evening meal until Kathryn's return. He'd told them it wasn't necessary but still they persisted in bringing him enough food for not only his evening meal but also to sustain him the next morning. It was Herman's wife who insisted he take his midday meal at her table. He was indeed blessed to have such good friends.

Just beyond the woman who was bringing his supper, he heard a commotion. Looking up, he saw Hunting Hawk coming toward them. Since everyone knew who he was and why he was there, no one questioned his arrival.

"I see the man you have been expecting has arrived. I will take your meal in and leave it on the table," the woman said.

Lukas nodded his approval of her plan and hurried to meet Hunting Hawk. His heart sank when he noticed the young man was alone.

"I do not bring you good news, Lukas," Hunting Hawk greeted him. "Wolf's Heart has said he will keep my mother and Sky Eyes as his slaves throughout the winter. When spring returns, he will release them but only for a ransom of four broken horses for each of them. Over this winter, I will be working with the men of my village in order to meet his price."

Lukas could feel his heart breaking with the news of not only Kathryn's but also Morning Star's fate. "Come to my house and take the evening meal with me. The women have been supplying me with food and there is always more than I can eat by myself. Once we have been refreshed ourselves, I will call a meeting of everyone. We must tell them what you have told me. They are more than anxious to be of help."

"Will they accept me?" Hunting Hawk inquired.

"I have been very honest with these people. They know all of Kathryn's background and are anxious to have her back among them. Here she is loved and respected more than she has been since she was a child in your village. I am certain they will be helpful."

Even though Lukas knew the food on his table was nothing familiar to Hunting Hawk, he ate with great relish and declared it good. With supper finished, they gathered the people together and told them of what Hunting Hawk came to tell them.

"We all want to help," Herman Kellogge declared. "There is a wild herd of horses not far from here. Over the winter, we will capture and break four horses as our portion of the ransom. Of course, we will leave them unshod."

Lukas watched Hunting Hawk's expression. He knew the young man was the same age as Kathryn but at that moment, he looked so much younger. He'd taken on the responsibility for not only his mother but the woman who'd grown up with him as his sister until they reached the age of fourteen.

"I do not know what to say," Hunting Hawk said in his faltering English.

"You need not say anything, my young friend," Herman replied. "Your sister is very important to everyone assembled here. We feel she is as much a part of our family as she is of yours."

Knowing Hunting Hawk might not completely understand what Herman said, he quickly translated the words into Hunting Hawk's language. He wondered if it was his imagination or if he actually saw unmanly tears in the young man's eyes.

~ * ~

The following morning, as soon as Hunting Hawk left the village, Lukas met with several of the men from the settlement to come up with a plan for raiding the wild herd of horses they knew to be just an hour's ride south of the settlement.

"Have you done this before?" Lukas asked.

He noticed several of the men nodding their heads.

It was an older man who stood to speak. "My name is Miles Howard. I have a farm outside of town where the horses can be housed and broken. When we first came here, we knew we would need more than the oxen we'd brought with us to pull our wagons. We had a few saddle horses, but there was a need for more. It was then we were told of the wild herd. We've gone there each year to add to our own horses plus to have some to sell. It won't be hard for us to do so again in order to get Kathryn returned to us."

Lukas held his tongue. He'd met Wolf's Heart and knew what a hard man he was. It was entirely possible once the ransom was paid, he would ask for more. He prayed his perception of the man was wrong, but at this point, the entire situation defeated him.

Along with the men from the settlement, he planned to find the wild herd for the following Saturday. By going to the herd before winter completely settled in, it would give them time to get the horses broken before Hunting Hawk's return in the spring.

~ * ~

The raid of the wild herd was a complete success. Not only did the men bring back the four horses for the ransom for Kathryn, but also another dozen horses to be distributed among the men who went with him. Lukas captured another two horses for himself, knowing full well it was possible Wolf's Heart could easily demand more horses than he originally asked for. If the man was content with the four horses, one could be given to Kathryn and the other to Hunting Hawk.

Once the horses were housed on Miles' farm, he made a suggestion Lukas found almost too good to be true. He said he had more land than he could handle alone. Since his son died during childhood and his daughter married and moved further west, he offered part of his land to Lukas as a farm of his own.

Only days after the raid on the wild herd, winter struck with a vengeance. Lukas was glad to be staying in Kathryn's house, within walking distance of the blacksmith shop. There was no lack of work and the hard labor kept his mind from wandering to what was happening in the Indian village where Kathryn was being held.

When he was not working for Herman, he made his way out to Mile's farm. Together they worked to break the horses and start building a house, barn, and corral that would make up Lukas' farm.

~ * ~

Hunting Hawk returned to his village, his heart heavy over the situation he'd left his sister and mother in, within the confines of Wolf's Heart's village.

Rather than stopping to see the whites who were living close to his village, Hunting Hawk rode directly to his home. The first person he met was Sly Coyote. He was hesitant about telling this man about the situation of the women of his family, since at one time everyone thought Sly Coyote and Sky Eyes would be married.

"You have been gone a long time, Hunting Hawk. What has kept you away from our village?"

"As you know, my mother wanted to see Sky Eyes. I took her to her white uncle only to be told she was no longer with them. It was the work of the Great Spirit that a man named Lukas was there. He is in love with my sister and told us where we could find her. Once we arrived at her new home, we learned Wolf's Heart had taken her as a slave. While we were there, my mother offered to take her place and now they are both his prisoners. I have returned home in the hopes of asking for the help of our people to raise the ransom of four horses Wolf's Heart requires for my mother."

"Four horses for your mother, but what does he request for Sky Eyes? Why are you not asking for help in gaining horses for her?"

"Lukas returned to where Sky Eyes has friends. They have agreed to provide the ransom for her. They respect and love her, unlike the people she ran from, both in this village and where she was living close to the big lake far to the east of us."

"I can't speak for everyone," Sly Coyote replied, "but I for one will not participate in such a fool's errand. Why would I want to raise a ransom for a white woman who is no longer of any use to our people? Perhaps you are foolish enough to continue to care for this white woman your parents tried to pass off as one of the people, but to me she is dead. As for your mother, she is no longer a productive member of our village. Younger women have taken her place. It is time she spent the winter with the horses and joined your father in walking with the ancestors."

Hunting Hawk remained silent for several moments in order to gain control of his temper. "I will not expect you to assist me in my quest. I will be speaking with the elders. If they are not in favor of this, I will take on the responsibility myself."

The expression on Sly Coyote's face told him he would probably not be getting help from his people. He knew his mother felt rejected, but he didn't think anyone else harbored the same feelings. From Sly Coyote's response, he knew there were others who would refuse to help him.

It took very little time for the elders to be assembled to listen to Hunting Hawk's plan.

"How do you know Wolf's Heart will honor the request for ransom once winter has ended?" Angry Otter asked. "You were foolish to leave your mother in his village."

"Her staying was not my idea, nor did I approve of it. My mother is a strong woman and she was the one who offered to stay instead of Sky Eyes. Unfortunately, Wolf's Heart is a hard man. He insisted both of them stay the winter in order to train several young women to be midwives. I know what a man like him is capable of. I will be willing to take not only four horses for my mother but an additional two horses. That should be enough for both of them when combined with the horses the people who live close to Sky Eyes will be providing."

"I considered both of your parents as my friends," Stalking Badger said, taking the floor. "Unfortunately, our people must prepare for the coming winter. Our hunters must provide for our needs. None of them can be spared to help you in your quest to obtain these horses. Your mother knew the consequences of leaving our people to go in search of this white woman. Neither of them is the obligation of the people any longer. I realize you think you are doing the best you can for your mother, but in this case, you must think of your people first. We need your excellence with a bow and arrow in order to feed our people."

"If that is your decision, I will hunt for the people, but I will also go in search of the wild horse herd. I will capture and break the horses Wolf's Heart has requested. Once my mother is freed from his village, we will find another village where the elders are not so judgmental of the elderly."

Without waiting for an answer, Hunting Hawk stormed from the council lodge and made his way to the lodge of his mother. Here he would stay, helping the hunters in their quest for food, but once he had the horses he needed, he would go south to the settlement where Lukas as well as Sky Eyes found friends as well as refuge.

~ * ~

Thomas was surprised to see Hunting Hawk return after being gone such a short time. The last time he'd seen the young man was when he came in search of Kathryn with his mother. This time, he came alone.

"Hunting Hawk, you are welcome in our home."

"Thank you. I have come for more than one reason. When I was here with my mother we came in search of my sister. It was Lukas who took us to where she was living. Once we arrived, we learned Sky Eyes had been taken to the village of a man named Wolf's Heart who now holds her as his slave. He also holds my mother, Morning Star. I returned to my people in the hopes of gaining their help in capturing the horses necessary for the ransom he requires to set my mother free, but they have denied me their help."

Thomas felt as though he'd been punched in the gut. How could his beautiful niece be a slave? "You speak of a ransom for your mother, but what of Kathryn? What is required in order for her to gain her freedom?"

"The people who she now calls her friends said they would supply the horses Wolf's Heart has required. I am responsible for those requested for my mother."

"If your people are not going to help you, will you be able to get the horses necessary for her ransom?"

"I hope I can get them, but my people also require me to hunt for them, so searching for the horses and breaking them will have to be done in addition to my obligations to my village."

"I am glad you came to us. I know there are people here who will be more than willing to help you with this. Many of us are indebted to your mother for saving Kathryn's life so many years ago. How many horses has he requested?"

"He has asked for four horses but I plan to bring him six. I know the man well enough to know he would probably not honor the original request."

"Do not worry about how to obtain the horses you need. Return to us in three days' time, and by then we will have formulated a plan to help you get the horses you need."

The smile on the young man's face said much more than any words he could have uttered. Ever since meeting Morning Star and others of her people, he'd come to highly respect them. The news of their rejection of Hunting Hawk's plea for help worked to change his mind. How could any people who once considered Morning Star a friend refuse to help to gain her freedom?

~ * ~

Hunting Hawk knew as soon as he went to Sky Eyes' white uncle to ask for help, his own people would no longer want him in the village. It didn't take long for them to tell him he was no longer welcome because he went to the people they considered to be their enemy.

With sadness in his heart he dismantled his mother's lodge and took it to a place in the forest not far from where the white man named Thomas lived. Once he established his new home, he went out in search of the herd of wild horses.

Three days later, he returned to meet with Thomas and the others. He was determined to not allow these white men know he was no longer living in the village. He needed their help to get the horses he needed, but he didn't want them to know how his people had turned their backs on him. It was bad enough he now felt as Sky Eyes must have felt when the people didn't want anything more to do with her.

As soon as he rode into the dooryard of Thomas' farm, the man hurried to greet him. "I am pleased to see you return to us. This is Marcus. He is Lukas' brother. He along with several other of the men are ready to go with you to the wild herd."

"I am grateful to you. I had hoped my people would be the ones to help me and they have disappointed me."

"What do your people say about you coming to us for help?"

Hunting Hawk was torn. In all of his life he had never told a lie to anyone. "I am no longer residing in the village. I have established my lodge in the forest, close to where I know the wild horses are."

It was Markus who reacted first. "How could your own people not want to help you? I was with Thomas when we first met your mother and again when my brother took the two of you to find Kathryn. Your mother is a very strong woman and I admire her. I'm honored to think you have enough trust in us to ask us for help. I have been thinking of raiding the wild herd for my own farm. Are you ready to leave?"

Even though Hunting Hawk's English was not perfect, he had no trouble in understanding the brother of his friend, Lukas. These whites were not as bad as his people always thought them to be.

It was Thomas who touched his shoulder, causing him to turn to face the older man. "I do not like the idea of you living alone in the forest. There are too many dangers there. Would you consider moving closer to us?"

Thomas' offer came as a surprise. Even though Hunting Hawk had been in two of the white man's towns, he didn't know if he could stand to live in one of the boxes the white men called home.

"I don't know if I could live in a box like you do."

"Perhaps I didn't say this correctly. What I meant was would you be willing to move your lodge to the outskirts of town. I have talked to Marcus and he has agreed to keep the horses at his farm. Give me time to talk to him. It is possible he would allow you to erect your lodge on his land."

Hunting Hawk watched as Thomas turned to Marcus. They spoke quietly between themselves. As they did, he tried to understand what Thomas meant when he called the land where Marcus lived, his land. To Hunting Hawk the land was just that, the land. It did not belong to anyone. It was there to be lived upon and used, but not to be owned.

Thomas returned to Hunting Hawk's side. "Marcus agrees with me. It is not good for you to be living alone. He would be pleased to have you living on his farm. It would give you a place to work with the horses we get from the wild herd. You would not only be training your horses, but we would all appreciate it if you could help train our horses. To be truthful, we're farmers and tradesmen. We usually buy our horses from others, we know nothing of how to break a horse. You would be doing us a great favor."

CHAPTER FIFTEEN

Winter snows fell daily and held the entire village in its grip. Kathryn as well as Morning Star now resided in the midwives' lodge and rarely left. The only exception was seeing to their bodily needs. With snow covering the ground, they were unable to search the forest for healing herbs. Although nothing was said, they knew they were guarded day and night. If it had not been for the women who were grateful for the way they were treated while giving birth, the two of them would have starved. Meals were brought to them on a daily basis and adequate clothing was provided.

Kathryn was beginning to wonder if Wolf's Heart knew of the kindness extended to them by the young mothers. Since the cold weather held the village in its grip, neither of them had seen any of the men from the village other than those who guarded the midwives' lodge.

"I am so sorry you have had to become a slave because of me, Mother."

"I do not regret my decision. Once the ransom Wolf's Heart has demanded is brought, I will no longer be able to be in your company."

"I do not see a reason why we should be separated again. It is not so far from the village to my new home."

"It is a long story. Due to this weather, we have plenty of time to tell it. When your father passed on to walk with the ancestors, it was evident it would not be much longer before the people no longer needed me. The decision came at the beginning of summer when I was told there were many young midwives and I would no longer be needed to help the women with the birthing of the babies born to the people. It was then I told your brother

I wanted to see you one last time."

"I have heard stories of women not being provided for once their husbands die, but couldn't Hunting Hawk hunt for you?"

"Of course he could, but the pull of seeing you was too strong. When this is over, my presence will no longer be necessary in the village."

"If that becomes reality, you will stay with me. The people living close to me are very understanding and loving. I am certain they will welcome you with open arms."

Kathryn wondered if she spoke the truth to her mother. She'd been very secretive about her past life. No one knew she'd been raised in an Indian village. They had no idea she could communicate with the people they considered savages. Even though she was white it was possible they wouldn't want her in their midst.

As much as she loved Lukas, she secretly wished the ransom would not be met. Once people knew about her past it was possible they would shun him and force them to move on. If that were to happen, she would never forgive herself.

A scratching at the door flap brought Kathryn from her mental musings. Once she answered it, she saw a young woman, Spotted Fawn, requesting entrance. Seeing her there, Kathryn knew it was time for her child to be born. Between herself and her mother they had been following the progress of her pregnancy. With her was one of the young women who had been training to become a midwife.

"I have been feeling the pains. I knew it was time for you to come for the birthing of my baby."

"Indeed, you are right," Kathryn said. "We will make you comfortable and before you know it, your child will be born."

While Kathryn reassured the young mother, the younger midwife helped Morning Star to prepare the birthing bed.

After checking over the expectant mother, Kathryn realized it was very early in the labor and the birth would not occur until late in the evening. It was entirely possible tonight she would be spending a sleepless night, but that didn't matter. He main focus was helping the young woman to bring forth a healthy baby.

Several hours later the sound of a newborn's cry filled the lodge. Kathryn held the tiny bundle of new life. As she did, she wondered if she would ever hold her own child. If she remained a slave in Wolf's Heart's village, it was a possibility he would arrange a marriage for her, perhaps even as a second wife to one of the elders. If that were to happen, she knew she would, more than likely, take her own life. To live in a loveless union was more than she could abide.

~ * ~

Lukas found the trip to the wild herd an exhilarating experience. He'd never broken a horse, but there were several others who knew the proper way to handle the task. In all, they'd brought twenty horses back to the settlement. In addition to the four to be taken to the Indian village and the two extra Lukas insisted he needed in case Wolf's Heart changed his mind, the farmers and townspeople who came along brought back the remaining fourteen for their own use or to be sold.

He'd asked to be a part of every bit of the operation. It didn't take long for him to learn the technique of catching the wild horses but breaking them was another thing. After being thrown several times, he finally mastered it.

Although he left the horses to be taken to Wolf's Heart's village unshod, he worked tirelessly in the blacksmith shop shoeing the horses of the other men in the village.

Each evening he returned to the house he'd planned to share with Kathryn, tired from a long day at work, but knowing he was one day closer to spring, when Hunting Hawk would return and they would make the trip to bring Kathryn back to the settlement.

Throughout the winter, with the help of his new friends and neighbors, Lukas was able to build a house, barn and corral. It was possible he wouldn't be able to work the land for yet another year, but it would give him and Kathryn a home of their own,

"Even though the snow is still on the ground, I saw a flock of geese flying to the north," Herman said one morning, when Lukas came into the shop to begin the day.

"I saw them also. I pray spring will soon be upon us. I can hardly wait to have Kathryn back in my arms. I can only pray these people will be accepting of her when she returns."

"You must know they will be. She has been missed, but thankfully, there have been none of the women who require her services during the winter. Are you planning to take any of the men with you when you deliver the horses?" Herman asked.

"I'm not sure. It will depend on whether or not Hunting Hawk brings men he trusts with him. I think Wolf's Heart will be more receptive to people of his own race than too many whites making the trip to his village. I am just so torn as to how this will all play out. Wolf's Heart and I did not make a good impression on each other at our first meeting."

Herman returned to building up the fire and Lukas also prepared to begin the day of working in the shop. As he did, he considered what would happen once Hunting Hawk finally arrived.

~ * ~

Hunting Hawk contemplated the journey he would be making to the south as soon as the snow was gone from the ground.

Along with many of the white men, he'd found the wild herd and brought back many more horses than was required in order to free his mother from Wolf's Heart's village. Throughout the winter, he'd taught his new-found friends how to break the horses. Even though he left his horses unshod, he appreciated learning how to shoe horses from Marcus.

Throughout the winter, he enjoyed having his lodge close to Marcus' home. With his new friend's help, he learned more of the English language and tried the foods Marcus' wife often brought to his lodge. He also hunted and provided venison as well as small game and birds for their table.

Never in his life did he think he would ever call a white man friend, but these people were really no different than the one-time friends he'd left behind in the village. They loved their families and treasured their friends.

~ * ~

Being confined to the midwives' lodge, Kathryn heard the sounds of the coming spring rather than seeing them. With all her heart, she prayed to both the Great Spirit and the God of the whites that throughout the winter Wolf's Heart's heart would have softened and they would be allowed to leave this village.

On her trip to the area where the women went to relieve themselves, Kathryn could smell spring in the early morning air. Even though stubborn patches of snow clung to the north side of the lodges, she knew it wouldn't be long before Hunting Hawk returned with the horses Wolf's Heart requested.

Before she made her way back to the lodge she shared with her mother, she saw Meadowlark hurrying toward her.

"I am so excited to see you," Meadowlark greeted her. "I was planning to come to your lodge later today. I am carrying Wolf's Heart's child. I think it will be born at the time of the harvest. I am so pleased to think you are in the village and will be able to help me with the birth."

Kathryn felt her heart sink. She considered Meadowlark to be her best friend in the village, even though she'd seen little of her over the winter. "It is possible I might not be here."

"What are you saying?"

"You must know Wolf's Heart has requested a ransom for both Morning Star and me. With spring coming, I am certain Hunting Hawk and Lukas will return to the village with the horses your husband has requested."

She could see tears forming in Meadowlark's eyes. "If you are gone, who will help me birth my baby?"

"You know there are several young women in this village who have been training to become midwives instead of my mother and me."

"I am afraid you are mistaken. Wolf's Heart told me when your brother and your man come, he plans to ask for more horses than he originally requested. When they are unable to meet his price, you will have to stay here."

Kathryn couldn't help the tears spilling from her eyes. "You remember what it was like when Jed took you away from your people and forced himself on you. I helped you to reunite with the man you love. Can you not do the same thing for me? I love Lukas. Had I known what was going to happen I would have never gone with Jed. I thought I would be returned to my home long before Lukas came to make me his wife. I long to be in his arms, just as you longed for Wolf's Heart to become your husband. I cannot continue to be a slave in this village. I miss my friends and my home."

"I don't know if anything I might say will sway Wolf's Heart but I will try. I will not be happy about your leaving, but I do know where your heart belongs and it is not within this village."

CHAPTER SIXTEEN

Lukas enjoyed the southerly breezes that promised spring would not be far away. Throughout the winter, in addition to his duties at the blacksmith shop, he made the trip out to the farms to care for the horses he would be taking to the Indian village.

"I'm going to miss these beauties," Miles said. "I don't know how I can ever thank you for allowing me to care for them through the winter. All of the horses we brought back to the settlement and our farms are prime stock. I've already had several offers for the ones I claimed for myself."

"Are you planning on selling your stock?"

"Not this year. I have put the stallion and the mares together and they will be giving me several colts before the snow flies in the fall. I've been talking to my wife and although the farming here is good, I need to have more than the crops and the milk from the cows. I'd like to start a breeding program. I have several mares I want to breed with the stallion. In time, I feel I could have quite an operation."

"I hope you haven't bred any of my mares."

"You know I haven't. I've kept your horses separate from the others. I have enjoyed watching you with them. You've learned how to break the horses and for that I am very proud of you. I was wondering, if I could go with you when you go to the Indian village. I know you've turned down the help of others, but I wouldn't go into the village with you. I would just go along to help with the horses during the time it takes to ride between here and there. I would also bring along two of my horses for Kathryn and her mother. If you are right, this man who holds them will end up taking every one of your horses."

"I'm afraid you are correct. I would be honored for you to come with us, but what of your farm?"

"I've talked to my brother and he has agreed to help my wife with the chores. I remember when my wife's niece was having trouble giving birth and it was Kathryn who helped her. It's the least I can do for one of our own."

Hearing Miles refer to Kathryn as one of their own warmed Lukas' heart. He never envisioned himself being anywhere other than on a farm bordering his brother's land. Over the few short months of winter, he'd found a life far away from the farm he'd always dreamed of, as well as having made good friends.

Kathryn running away from Amy's accusations had given them both a new life. He could only pray he would be allowed to bring her back as his wife.

~ * ~

"You've been a good friend and neighbor throughout this winter," Marcus said to Hunting Hawk while they worked with the horses on the first warm day of spring. "Thomas and I have decided to go south with you when you take the horses to Wolf's Heart."

Hunting Hawk was caught completely off guard. Had he heard Marcus correctly? "How can you leave here? You have told me how spring is a busy time for you on your farm."

"There are others in the community who have offered to help with my spring chores. I am anxious to see not only my brother but also Kathryn. As for Thomas, you know he is Kathryn's uncle and he is also anxious to see her. There are others here who are capable of helping out in the store as well as his oldest son. We have settled these things among ourselves and only need your approval of our plan."

Again, Hunting Hawk was overwhelmed by the generosity of these white strangers who had become his friends. When his own people turned their backs on him, they offered him land to raise his lodge and helped him in his quest to gain the horses Wolf's Heart requested.

~ * ~

The days became warmer and, as they did, he scanned the horizon daily looking for Hunting Hawk to arrive with his share of the horses.

It was just after the first of April when one of the young boys came to the blacksmith shop with the news he and his friend saw three men with a bunch of horses riding toward town. He said they'd been on their way home from school and he was sure one of the men was the Indian who came to find Lukas last fall.

"This is what you've been waiting for," Herman said. "It's time to close up for the day. If we work together we can get it done and then ride out to meet Hunting Hawk."

"That sounds good. I wonder who the other men with him are. I know he was hoping some of the men from his village might come with him. I'm anxious to meet them."

It didn't take long to close down the shop and for Herman and Lukas to saddle their horses for the ride out of town.

Lukas immediately recognized Hunting Hawk but was shocked to see Marcus and Thomas riding with him. As soon as he realized his brother was coming to him, he spurred his horse to a gallop to close the distance between the two of them.

"I can't believe you're here," Lukas said as he clasped his brother's hand. "I thought Hunting Hawk would be bringing men from his village with him."

"That's a long story, brother," Marcus replied. "Is there somewhere we can put the horses for the night? Do you have room for us in your home?"

"I can make room. As for the horses, Miles Howard has been holding the ones I claimed. He will be going with us when we leave for Wolf's Heart's village. We will be able to take your herd there."

With all of the horses that would be taken to the Indian village, together in the paddock at Miles' farm, Lukas rode back into town with his three houseguests. While Kathryn's house was small, it could easily accommodate the men who were more than willing to sleep on the floor in bedrolls. He wished he could have taken all of them to his new home, but he didn't want to move in until he could do so with Kathryn by his side.

The evening meal was provided by more than one woman. Everyone was anxious to help out in the hopes of seeing Kathryn's return to their midst.

For Lukas, being reunited with both his brother and Thomas was an added blessing. Over supper they discussed the plan for delivering the horses. It was agreed they would go together to where Lukas and Hunting Hawk camped before riding the short distance to the village. There, Markus, Thomas and Miles would wait while Lukas and Hunting Hawk delivered the eight horses. If indeed Wolf's Heart asked for more horses, Lukas would ride back to bring the other four horses into the village.

~ * ~

Early the next morning, many residents met in the village square to bid the party taking the ransom to the Indian village a safe journey.

"We wish you well," Caroline Peters said. "Please tell Kathryn how much I've missed her this past winter. I've talked to several of the other women and they are excited to be welcoming Morning Star as another midwife. I know you've been building a house out on your farm, so that will leave Kathryn's house empty. I pray Morning Star will agree to live there and be with us when it is our time of giving birth."

"I will tell both of them," Lukas promised. "I'm sure Kathryn has missed you as well. When we return, it will be a time for celebration."

Lukas wondered if there would be a celebration or if Wolf's Heart would go back on his promise to accept the ransom he'd requested. With all his heart, he prayed Wolf's Heart would be a man of his word.

Sky Eyes

~ * ~

As it had been the first time Lukas and Hunting Hawk traveled to the village with Morning Star, the going was slow. It was only right not to run the horses too hard.

When at last they arrived at the area where they'd camped the night before they'd gone to the village in the hopes of rescuing Kathryn, Lukas noticed the difference from six months earlier. Instead of the dried grasses of late summer, there was the lush new growth of spring. It pleased him to think there would be good grazing for the horses.

It took little time to picket the horses and to establish their camp. With the excitement of once again seeing Kathryn, Lukas found sleep to be a stranger. Hoping to leave camp without bothering the other men, he slipped away and stood on the bank of the small stream that bordered their camp.

"Would you like some company, brother?" he heard Marcus say from behind him.

"I welcome your company, but I thought you were sleeping."

"I doubt any of us are sleeping this night. The thought of reuniting you and Kathryn as well as Hunting Hawk and his mother has us all on edge."

Lukas nodded, knowing in the light of the full moon his brother could see his gesture. "What if Wolf's Heart has forced her into a marriage over the winter? As his slave, he could demand such a thing. Will she still be willing to come with me?"

"You are talking foolishly. Didn't you tell me how Wolf's Heart had come to claim the woman he loved even though she had been sold to a white man? What kind of a man would put you in the same situation because you have come for the woman you love and have brought the ransom he demanded for her release? I feel you worry for no reason. Tomorrow will be here before we know it, so it is best if we both go back to our bedrolls and try to get a little sleep."

Lukas agreed and followed his brother back to camp. Although Marcus made sense, he still harbored concerns about what the morning would bring.

~ * ~

Kathryn finished her morning ritual of bathing in the stream beside the village and taking care of her bodily needs. The warmth of the spring morning prompted her to gather the young women who were training with her to go into the forest in search of spring roots and herbs.

When she arrived at the midwives' lodge, she was surprised to see Wolf's Heart waiting for her.

"Is there something I can do for you?" she asked.

"I was told you are gathering together the women who have been training with you. I do not want you going into the forest today."

Anger built within her. "I have been your slave for almost an entire year. Do you think I would run away now? The women I have been training have become my friends. Even though they know which plants and roots to harvest, I am looking forward to time away from this lodge where you have kept me prisoner for the entire winter. I need fresh air and sunshine, as does my mother."

"I know you call Morning Star your mother and I have heard the story of how she raised you when your white parents were gone, but you must know a white woman could never be one with the people. Besides, my scouts have told me the white man named Lukas and Hunting Hawk have arrived with the horses I demanded. They have brought three white men with them."

"Lukas is here? Are you going to allow me to leave with them?"

"It depends on the condition of the horses they brought with them. I know I asked for four horses for you and four horses for Morning Star but you have become so valuable to me I plan to request six horses for each of you."

"That's not fair and you know it," Kathryn spat. "How can you change the agreed upon amount at this late date? There is no way they can catch, gentle, and break four extra horses."

"That is the idea, my dear. You will be my slave until I say you can leave and not before. If they cannot meet my new terms, they will be the ones to lose, because you will remain my slave. Perhaps someday soon I will take you as a second wife. I am certain you know my wife, Meadowlark, is carrying my child. That said, I have no one to warm my bed and I think you could do that quite nicely."

Anger exploded as Kathryn brought up her hand to slap Wolf's Heart's face. As soon as her palm connected with his cheek, he retaliated by slapping her so hard she fell backward twisting her ankle.

"You have no idea what you have just done. As a slave, I could order you killed, but I am not a cruel captor."

Before she could make a smart retort, a commotion came from the people in the village. Unable to pick herself up from the ground, she saw Hunting Hawk and Lukas enter the village, each leading four horses. From what she could tell from her vantage point, she could see they were prime stock.

"We have come for my mother and sister," Hunting Hawk announced. "We have fulfilled your request for four horses for each woman."

"Things have changed. These women have become very important to our village. If you want them, you will bring four more horses to my village. I warn you, they must be gentled and broken, just like the ones you have brought today."

Kathryn could feel her heart sink. She knew it would take several months for the new request to be fulfilled. Just as she thought all hope was gone, she saw Lukas put two fingers into his mouth and emit a shrill whistle.

From the direction Lukas and Hunting Hawk had come, another man, leading another four horses, rode into the village. She was shocked to see it was her Uncle Thomas.

"We anticipated you would change the details of your deal," Lukas said.

His mastery of her language came as a surprise.

"That being the case, we have each brought six horses. If you do not want your people to think you are out to cheat us, you will release Kathryn and Morning Star."

Kathryn took a moment to look at Wolf's Heart. His expression was one of disbelief. She was certain no one had ever anticipated his moves and outsmarted him before.

Unable to back down, he stepped aside so Lukas could dismount and rush to her side.

"Has he injured you?" Lukas said, as he helped her to her feet and she winced in pain.

"I – I twisted my ankle and fell."

"There is a red mark on your face in the shape of a man's hand. Did Wolf's Heart hit you?"

Tears flowed from her eyes. "I struck him in anger. He only retaliated. I want no more trouble with the people of this village. Please say nothing more about this. I just want to go home."

In the confusion, she didn't see Hunting Hawk going to the midwives' lodge to bring Morning Star out for them to return home.

She also saw Miles Howard and Lukas' brother Marcus ride into the village. They each led an extra horse.

"We are prepared to take my mother and sister with us," Hunting Hawk announced. "You have twelve new horses, all of them gentled and broken. You will now allow us to take them away from your village. Should you try to follow us or seek retaliation we will not be responsible for our response to you."

To Kathryn's surprise, it was Meadowlark who came to step between her husband and Hunting Hawk.

"You will abide by the original agreement," she said through clinched teeth. "Only a dishonest man would change the request without warning. I know you are not a dishonest man, my husband. I fear you are doing this in retaliation for what Jed did to you. You are not being fair. Tell these men you will take the four horses for each woman as was agreed upon. If you do not, there will not be a man or woman in this village who will respect you again."

Wolf's Heart turned to Hunting Hawk. "My wife speaks the truth. Sky

Eyes and Morning Star have spent the winter training our young women to be midwives. They have more than paid the ransom. I will take two horses and only two horses. The rest you can take back with you. I wanted revenge but my wife is right, I took out my anger on the wrong people. I pray the Great Spirit will forgive me."

Kathryn allowed Lukas to lift her into his arms and walk toward the waiting horses.

"Give her to me, so you can mount your horse," Thomas said. "Since I can see she is injured, I am certain you want her riding in front of you on the way back to camp."

Kathryn's resolve dissolved as soon as Thomas took her from Lukas. Any control she'd had since becoming Wolf's Heart's slave left and she began to sob uncontrollably.

"I can't believe you came back for me," she said, reaching out to touch Lukas' hand.

"I told Wolf's Heart you were my woman. I love you and I refuse to ever let you go again. As soon as we get back to the settlement I plan to ask the minister to make us man and wife."

The thought of going back to her previous home suddenly made Kathryn uneasy. "I know these people know where I've been, but what if they learn about my past?"

"They know and they want you no matter what. Not everyone is like Amy. These are good people. They have missed you."

Kathryn glanced at her brother. Something about him seemed different to her.

"I, too, have been living among the whites," he said in his native language. "Our people no longer welcome me in our village. When they turned their backs on me, I knew how you felt. If it were not for your uncle and Lukas' brother, I don't know what I would have done. I was able to erect my lodge on the land Marcus calls his farm. We have learned much from each other over the winter. He has told me I am welcome to continue to live on his farm and help him. He and others helped to catch the horses."

"With five horses, you are now a very wealthy man. Will you be content to remain on the land the whites have claimed? Will you not want to return to the people?"

"The people no longer want me. I have found acceptance and friendship with Marcus and the other people of the settlement. They are good people. As for being rich, I am hoping to be able to breed my mares. Marcus says since I am so good with horses, we will make a good team and be able to sell them to make a good living. I know it's different from the way we were brought up, but it is a life I am coming to enjoy."

Thomas moved toward Lukas now that he'd mounted his horse. "Please allow me to bid my friend Meadowlark farewell."

Thomas waited while the young woman approached Kathryn.

"I will miss you, my friend," Kathryn said.

"I will miss you as well. Thank you for training those of us who want to be midwives. I know I will be in good hands when the time comes for my baby to be born. You will always be welcome in my lodge."

Kathryn reached up to wipe away the tears that had once again begun to fall. As Meadowlark backed away, Thomas lifted her up to Lukas' waiting arms.

Once seated comfortably in front of Lukas, she looked back to see her mother mount one of the horses Hunting Hawk brought with them.

Her last glimpse of the village where she'd spent the winter months, was seeing the women bidding her farewell. She'd made good friends here and certainly didn't want to ever forget any one of them.

~ * ~

Secure in Lukas' embrace, she saw where the men camped the night before. She prayed they wouldn't stop there as it was too close to Wolf's Heart's village. It was entirely possible he might try to follow them to take her back.

"You don't trust Wolf's Heart, do you?" Lukas asked.

Kathryn shook her head. "I fear he will go back on his word. I want as much distance between his village and us as possible before we stop for the night."

"You have no need to worry. We have enough men to keep you and Morning Star safe. If we make good time, we will be back home before you know it."

Kathryn relaxed and allowed the movement to the horse to lull her into a peaceful sleep. When she again awoke, the horse had slowed and she saw the men working to make camp. Having come to Wolf's Heart's village from Jed's cabin, she had no idea how far she had traveled away from her beloved home.

"Do you think we are safe to stop? There is still daylight."

"The horses need to rest and we need time to do some hunting for our evening meal. I also want Morning Star to look at your ankle. I pray it isn't injured too badly."

Kathryn knew from the throbbing of her ankle, even when it didn't touch the ground, she had injured it. Her mother would know what to do to heal it quickly.

The stopping place was several hours journey from the village to their now erected camp but Kathryn still worried about the possibility of them being followed. Even though Wolf's Heart gave his word he would not pursue them, she had her doubts. He'd told her she would be returned to her friends once Meadowlark and her baby were out of danger, but he hadn't kept his word.

Rather than dwell on Wolf's Heart and his broken promises, Kathryn turned her attention to Morning Star and her examination of her ankle.

"It is not badly injured," Morning Star declared. "I can see there is bruising and swelling, but nothing is broken. There is a fast running stream close by. I will ask Lukas to take you there so you can soak your foot in the cold water. By morning you will be able to walk on it even though it will still be painful."

Morning Star hoisted herself to her feet and went to where Hunting Hawk was skinning the two rabbits he'd killed for their evening meal.

"I heard what your mother told you," Lukas said, as he helped her to her feet before lifting her in his arms. "I think it's time you take care of yourself. I would also like to soak my feet in the stream."

Even though Kathryn knew she should be helping her mother, she put those thoughts aside and enjoyed the feeling of being protected in Lukas' arms. Throughout her time in Wolf's Heart's village, Lukas' proclamation of love while standing in her house and calling her 'his woman' in the village, kept her going. She prayed yet another long winter of being separated had not quenched the love he professed.

"Before I left, I asked the parson to join us in marriage upon our return. I know you will want Thomas with you as much as I want Marcus with me. They have both agreed to remain with us until we are man and wife. I also know Hunting Hawk's feelings about this. He too would like to see you safely married and settled."

The mention of Hunting Hawk brought a new dread to her mind. "Do you think it's a good idea for the people to know of my connection to Hunting Hawk and Morning Star?"

"Everyone in the village knows and respects both your mother and your brother. I have been asked if I thought Morning Star would remain once we return so she can help you when you are called upon to attend the women who are having babies. Since you left, there are many young families moving in. The people can see the need for more than one midwife."

"Where will she live?"

"Over the winter, I built us a new house. It's on the outskirts of town and I had hoped to raid the wild herd for more horses and begin breeding and selling saddle and work horses. With the five horses I'm bringing back with me, I will be able to establish my business sooner rather than later."

"What of your job with Herman Kellogge? Are you not still working in his blacksmith shop?"

"Of course I am. In addition to that, our farm is next to the one where Miles and his wife live. Miles and I are going to become partners in the horse breeding business. He, too, went with us to the wild herd and brought back horses for himself. He has two fine stallions and two mares who are now bred. Add to that the stallion and the mares I am bringing back, we will be able to start selling stock in two years. In the meantime, we will have our work at the shop to keep us going. It will be a perfect solution for both of us."

"Do you think Hunting Hawk will join you?"

She watched as Lukas' brows knotted, as though he was in deep thought. "Miles and I both asked him the same thing. He told us he is not ready to be so far away from the people of his village. He and my brother have entered into the same agreement as Miles and me. He raised his lodge on my brother's land and throughout the winter they worked the horses together. Now that he has the extra five horses to their herd, he will be able to help with the breeding and training of not only Marcus' stock but those of his own."

Even though she still had apprehensions about returning, Kathryn realized she needed to become more accepting and less worried about the people she called friends. If they still wanted her, knowing of her background, she knew things would be the same as they'd been before she went with Jed to attend Meadowlark as she gave birth. So much had happened since then, she was more than ready to return to her happy life along with her new husband.

CHAPTER SEVENTEEN

The night before they were due to arrive, Hunting Hawk insisted they make camp one last time. Once they were settled, Miles rode ahead to tell everyone of the good news of the rescue of Kathryn and Morning Star.

Even though everyone else talked incessantly about Morning Star staying with them, Kathryn still harbored doubts. The memory of the stories spread about her by Amy were still foremost in her mind. What if the people here felt the same way about her upbringing as Amy had? Would they turn on her as well as the woman she'd called mother for the majority of her life?

"It looks like you're deep in thought," Lukas said as he seated himself next to her by the campfire.

"I'm just worried. What if the people I've called friends turn their backs on me?"

Lukas laughed. "I wouldn't worry about such a thing if I were you. How many times must I tell you? Everyone knows about your background and they are all looking forward to your return. Since you have been gone, there are many new families moving into the area. I've spoken with several people and they all agree your mother would be welcome to become a second midwife. These people aren't like Amy. They know and love you and having met your mother last fall they are anxious to welcome her into their midst."

Kathryn breathed a little easier. Just the thought of seeing the people she called friends again made her relax. Over the winter, she'd lived the life she'd grown up living. At the same time, she missed the house where she lived. It amazed her how easily she'd adapted to the white ways.

Kathryn spent a sleepless night. Her excitement about returning home kept sleep from her restless mind.

At long last, the sun crested the eastern horizon signaling the beginning of a new day. Kathryn was the first of the group to stir. Anxious to return to her home, she was already preparing the morning meal when the others awoke from their slumber.

Once the morning meal was finished, they mounted their horses and headed toward the place where both she and Lukas would now call home.

~ * ~

Caroline Peters worked feverishly with the other women in preparing the food for the celebration of Kathryn's return to them. She'd even taken it upon herself to check out the house where Kathryn lived before becoming a prisoner in Wolf's Heart's village. Even though she knew Lukas lived there all winter, she doubted he had the determination to keep the house as clean as Kathryn did.

As she swept the floor, she thought about the woman who might be living there. With Lukas' house on his property, Kathryn would no longer be living in town. The house and its furnishings would belong to Morning Star.

She'd met Morning Star in the fall. Even though they hadn't been able to communicate, Caroline knew they could easily become good friends. With her own mother no longer alive, she would enjoy having the older woman as one of her close neighbors.

"Miles said they should be here shortly after noon," Milly Jamison said, as she helped Caroline set up the long table where the food would soon be spread. "I have my beans ready and I see several of the other women are bringing out their specialties. I hope Morning Star and Hunting Hawk will like them."

Caroline smiled. "I'm certain they will. After traveling the distance from Wolf's Heart's village, I think they will appreciate everything we are preparing."

A commotion from the other side of town ended their conversation. Caroline looked up to see Kathryn and Lukas leading their party, along with almost as many horses as they had taken with them, into the village. Excited to see her friend, Caroline left what she was doing and hurried to be one of the first people to greet them.

"Caroline," Kathryn called, as she dismounted and ran the short distance between the horses and her friend.

Caroline couldn't help the tears that were streaming down her cheeks. "Oh, Kathryn, I have worried so about you. Were you able to keep warm throughout the winter? Did they give you enough to eat?"

"The answers to your questions are yes, and yes. I'm afraid the dress I was wearing when I came to your house to tell you I was going with Jed did not last me through the winter, but the lodge where I stayed was very warm. As for the food, the people provided me with the nourishment I needed."

For the first time, Caroline assessed the clothing Kathryn wore. Rather than a dress made from flax or wool, she wore one made of finely tanned buckskin. Her shoes had been replaced by a pair of knee high moccasins.

Turning her attention to the older woman in the party, she realized she wore similar attire. Having had little contact with Indians in the past, she'd given little thought to what they would wear. The buckskin dress looked more comfortable than the homespun, flax or wool dresses she wore.

"I was afraid that horrible man wouldn't let you go."

"It's a long story, Caroline. Wolf's Heart needed my help, but he had no idea how to ask for it. He thought he had to make me his slave in order to have women trained to be midwives. In the end, he demanded six horses rather than the four he asked for last fall. It was his wife, Meadowlark, who shamed him in front of his people. Because of that he only took one horse from Lukas and one from my brother, Hunting Hawk. In the end, everything is working out. I am looking forward to becoming Lukas' wife and returning to all the friends I've made here."

Before Caroline could respond, the parson approached them.

"Miles came to me early this morning and said Lukas and Kathryn wish to be married."

Kathryn turned and saw Lukas standing with the parson.

"I thought this would be a good time for us to be joined together as man and wife, while your uncle and brother are still here with us."

"I-I don't know what to say. I don't have a proper dress."

Caroline began to smile. "Come to my house. I have just the dress for this occasion. It's the dress I wore on my wedding day and I know it will fit you perfectly."

~ * ~

Kathryn couldn't believe how so much could have happened in such a short period of time. Less than a week ago, she and her mother were slaves in Wolf's Heart's village. Now she was back in the place she called home where she had friends and she was preparing for her marriage to Lukas.

As much as she wanted to bask in the feeling of being back in her home with Morning Star, she knew she wanted her Uncle Thomas and Hunting Hawk at her wedding as much as Lukas wanted his brother, Marcus, there. If she were to say she needed more time would mean none of the people who were important in both of their lives would be there.

Reluctantly, she ran her hands over the buckskin dress Meadowlark had provided for her when the dress she'd been wearing ever since Wolf's Heart made her his slave was in tatters. Even though she knew the buckskin dress would remain in her possession, she wondered how it would feel to wear the constricting dress of the whites. In the past, she'd welcomed the style of the whites, but now she wondered in which of the two worlds she really belonged.

"Here it is," Caroline said, as she brought out the dress from the trunk where it had been stored.

Kathryn could only stand and stare at the beautiful cream colored dress Caroline held out to her. "Oh Caroline, this is much too beautiful. I'm not worthy to wear such a dress."

"That's nonsense if I ever heard it. You are one of the most beautiful women for miles around. I have water heating so you can wash the trail dust from your body. Once that is done, I'll help you put on the dress and style your hair. You will be the most beautiful bride anyone has ever seen. Now let's get started."

Kathryn followed Caroline into the kitchen where she'd had her husband bring in a bathing tub which she'd filled with warm water. As soon as she stepped into the water, Kathryn realized just how much she'd missed bathing in warm water. During the fall and spring, she'd been allowed to bathe in the stream with the other women. The water had always been cold and invigorating but never as comfortable as the warm water she'd become accustomed to using since becoming one with the white society.

After her bath, Kathryn felt much better. The grit of the dust from the journey away from slavery and back to freedom had been now washed away. For the first time, she contemplated the dress Caroline insisted she should wear for her wedding. The material was soft and silky to the touch.

"I have never felt anything like this before," Kathryn said, as Caroline slipped the dress over her head.

"My mother said it was a dress her mother had made for her before her marriage. She couldn't remember the type of fabric that was used, but she knew her parents were wealthy. They had a very prosperous farm in New York state. I'm saving it for my daughters to wear, but I'm honored to have you wear it for your wedding."

To hear Caroline say her parents came from New York brought to mind how her white family had also come from that place in the east. She decided it must be a wonderful place to live and be wealthy. Why anyone from there would venture into what was considered the wilderness was beyond her understanding.

~ * ~

Lukas always knew he would waste no time in making Kathryn his wife but things seemed to be moving too quickly. It was like he was reading one of the fairy stories he'd read to his nieces and nephews while he was in New York. While Kathryn prepared for the wedding, he took Morning Star to the house that would belong to her once he and Kathryn moved out to the farm and the home he'd built for her.

"I have never lived in a white man's house," Morning Star said, as soon as they walked the short distance to the house Lukas' had called his own over the winter.

"I think you will find it very comfortable, Mother," Hunting Hawk assured her. "Over the winter, I have often visited the home of Marcus and his wife. As I told you, we are no longer welcome in our village. These people have told Lukas they want you to stay with them and they will welcome your skills as a midwife. I know you will soon learn how to cook not only in the way of the white man, but to also enjoy the other furnishings in the house."

Lukas watched as Morning Star contemplated everything her son was telling her. Kathryn told him how, over the winter, she'd been teaching her mother to speak English. It was entirely possible she anticipated the actions of the people in the Indian village where she grew up.

"You are right, my son. On the journey from the village to here, you have told me of the treatment you have received at the hands of those we once called friends. I know this is my fault. Had I not taken Sky Eyes away from the sights and smells of death, we would still be welcomed among our people."

"Had you not taken Sky Eyes as your own, I would not have had her as my sister. Until she met her white family, I never considered her different from any of our friends. I grieve for the people who have turned their backs on us. They do not have an understanding of the good you did by saving her life. I told you how I went there to enlist the help of my friends and they refused to assist me. I have made a life for myself helping Marcus on his farm. With the horses I now have, I am a very rich man. Marcus and I have been talking about breeding horses and now I can contribute these to the business we plan to begin."

"You make me proud, just as Sky Eyes brings pride to me. I will try to adjust to the ways of the whites. I already feel wanted by these people. It saddens me that our own people no longer want us in their midst. This is a time for change and we will adapt to what fate has given us."

"Then you'll stay in this house?" Lukas asked.

"It will not be like my lodge but it will be comfortable. I am pleased these people want me to do what I do best. I will be happy here and I know my son will not be too far away from me. As for my daughter, I know she will be well loved as she will have a good man as her husband."

Lukas beamed at the compliment Morning Star gave him. It mattered not that she spoke in her native tongue rather than the English Kathryn told him she'd been learning. In either language her words were laced with love. During the time they'd been together, he'd come to admire both this woman and her son. How anyone could have ever called them dirty savages was beyond his comprehension.

~ * ~

By the time Kathryn left Caroline's house, the common area seemed to be deserted. As soon as they entered the church, she knew exactly where everyone was. All of the people she knew and had missed over the winter were gathered with the new families who recently moved in, and were seated on the long plank pews of the sanctuary.

Hunting Hawk waited for her at the back of the church while Lukas and Marcus stood at the front waiting for her to arrive. As her best friend, Caroline walked to the front of the church ahead of her.

The music provided by Miles Howard and Herman Kellogge on their fiddles accompanied her walk toward Lukas. The remainder of the service was a blur until the parson finally pronounced them man and wife.

The dreams she'd enjoyed all through the winter were coming true. She was accepted in a community who not only knew of her background but didn't shame her because of it.

About the Author

At the age of fifteen, Sherry Derr-Wille walked into her sophomore English class and fell in love with writing. Her teacher, Earl Brockman, "The Duke of Earl," announced that anyone getting an A on the first test could sit in the back of the room and write. Since no one ever told her to stop, she continued to write for over forty years before becoming published in 2003.

Married to her high school sweetheart, Bob, for over fifty years, she calls him a saint for putting up with a crazy writer. Together they raised three children, have nine grandchildren and five great-granddaughters.

Born a country girl, she loves living in a mid-sized city close to the Illinois border with Wisconsin. Being retired gives her time to follow her heart writing along with editing for several private clients and three publishers.

**VISIT OUR WEBSITE
FOR THE FULL INVENTORY
OF QUALITY BOOKS**:

http://www.roguephoenixpress.com

Rogue Phoenix Press
Representing Excellence in Publishing

*Quality trade paperbacks and downloads
in multiple formats,
in genres ranging from historical to contemporary romance,
mystery and science fiction.
Visit the website then bookmark it.
We add new titles each month!*

Made in the USA
Lexington, KY
15 March 2018